SOFTCORE

Tirdad Zolghadr is an independent critic and curator born in 1973. Aside from the field of contemporary art, Zolghadr has worked in journalism, translation and documentary film. He is also a founding member of the Shahrzad art & design collective.

Tirdad Zolghadr

Softcore

TELEGRAM

London   San Francisco   Beirut

ISBN 13: 978-1-84659-020-7

copyright © Tirdad Zolghadr 2007

This edition published 2007 by Telegram Books

A full CIP record for this book is available from the British Library
A full CIP record for this book is available from the Library of Congress

Manufactured in Lebanon

TELEGRAM
26 Westbourne Grove, London W2 5RH
825 Page Street, Suite 203, Berkeley, California 94710
Tabet Building, Mneimneh Street, Hamra, Beirut
www.telegrambooks.com

*My deepest thanks
to Charles Buchan
and Khavar Zolghadr*

Patronage

I'm standing in a side alley somewhere in downtown Tehran. On this February afternoon, I'm wearing a duffle coat over a polo shirt, blue jeans, tinted glasses, unfashionably lavish sideburns and a sparse, scruffy beard. Though actually much younger, I appear to be in my mid-thirties, underweight, short and slightly hunched, with striking, full lips and a Caesar's cut of red hair over a high forehead. Even if I'm actually rather sure of myself, I never fail to look self-conscious. I'm the type to make you wonder whether the difference between shyness and reserve, or charm and condescension, was as obvious as you'd always assumed. I'm nursing a hangover from a housewarming party the night before.

Before climbing into the taxi behind me I lean back, taking in the concrete façade on the other side of the street. Through the swinging glass doors on the ground floor I can make out a round, tube-like corridor, painted over in black-and-white zebra stripes. The winding corridor makes a sharp turn to the left, then immediately to the right, before slanting downwards, into a large salon which has remained unused for two decades.

The zebra motif continues across the walls of the salon and much of the furniture, including the Eames surfboard tables, the polyethylene chairs, and the barstools surrounding the circular chrome bar in the symmetric center of the room. The glaring stripes are soon to be replaced by untreated cement in varying shades, from dusky white to brute, concrete gray. An occasional sprinkle of designer neon, matched with a scattering of Turkoman pillows, early Safavid miniatures and black-and-white Qajar photography, will ensure just the right blend of ethnic marketing and cosmopolitan obeisance.

Upon arriving in Tehran the month before last, I quickly decided to re-open the family establishment, the Promessa, not as the restaurant and cocktail bar it once was but as a showroom of sorts, a space for art exhibitions, catwalks, launches, readings, screenings, student workshops, talks, corporate receptions, film sets, dance parties and such. The room is to remain mostly vacant, polyfunctional, presumptuous in its lavish use of space, displaying little at a time, when it's showing anything at all. Upstairs by the entrance is an unframed black-and-white portrait of Zsa Zsa, matron and matriarch who founded the Promessa some forty years ago.

There will be not one but two openings: an official vernissage early on a Wednesday afternoon, an unofficial one later the same day. The official opening shall be the more entertaining by far. Bureaucrats in loose-fitting gray suits, shapeless, gusty trousers flowing over cheap black leather shoes onto the floor. The government brand of canonical humility, of the people for the people, bulky glasses, and six-day stubble carefully trimmed. They'll be sipping on Fantas and smiling, always careful to take long, thoughtful, suggestive pauses before speaking.

Friends from the clergy will also be invited. Camel-fur capes, black turbans or white, gray and light-blue robes reaching down almost to the ground. The effect is superb. Mullahs always look like they're floating, hovering two inches above the floor. They, like the bureaucrats, choose their words carefully, but tend to speak in strenuous hypotheses and confident conclusions, not in candy-coated, officious formulae.

There will also be the art scene, or the official rendition thereof. National museums, international *cinéma d'auteurs*. And artists in Nike running shoes and CK shirts elaborating on their *instaaleshens*, and their *performaanses* to French reporters and Lebanese curators. And there could well be a reading. Your visiting journalist-writer with his written impressions of the country, paying homage to the particular, gentle allure of the luscious Persian melancholy, the cultivated religiosity and smiling self-denial that are brought to bear these days in Iran. And there should be celebrities, of a comfortably wide range, if possible. Anything from Neil Diamond to Michael Moore to someone more artworld. And there will also be my friend and mentor Stella.

Stella is a historian, specializing in postwar art brut, whom I met in the US some ten years ago. It would be hard to overestimate the impact Stella has had on my life, from my politics to my personal tastes to my everyday habits, none of which have remained untouched since that first, chance meeting at an espresso bar on Houston University Campus, following a lecture on Richard Greaves. Stella, with her limitless web of devoted artworld contacts, her impeccable sense of dress and the way she seems to have an answer to everything from the discrepancy between a latte machiatto and a latte *tout court* to conflicting histories of urban guerilla warfare in twentieth-century Chad.

Stella is an heir to old, mature money and has also been the only source of financial support for the showroom project to date, although this, she has made clear, is bound to change sooner or later. The fact is, despite her considerable standing in academia, I'd never heard of Stella until I was introduced to her by an old family friend, a certain Tan Christenhuber, or 'Uncle Tan', an oil engineer from Hamburg.

At the opening, I'm hoping Stella will offer her typical celebrations of Third World megalopoles as adorable swirls of plastic glitz, to then affront and galvanize with select historical revisionisms, cheap, brutal and unfair, reaping unending discussions with alternating bureaucrats sweetly smiling over their Fantas.

The unofficial opening: raisin vodka, a dozen entrées, crystal meth or second-rate cocaine in the restrooms, opium and sweet black tea in the back garden to impress Stella. Many associate opium with Lewis Carroll, dream-like euphoria and de Niro in *Once Upon a Time in America*. But the local variety offers a very mild effect, hardly more bewildering than a hot bath.

I turn and make for the cab, avoiding the patches of damp snow on the sidewalk. The driver nods and mumbles politely as he turns the key in the ignition. He's wearing a light gray polyester suit and looks like a young Leonid Brezhnev. Very much my idea of an essentially characteristic Russian (or Ukrainian, perhaps) – pale cheeks and dismal shadows under St Bernard eyes – which reminds me that Stella is to leave St Petersburg next week and will soon, hopefully, be flying on to Tehran.

The driver switches on the tape recorder, to what sounds like Neil Diamond, live in concert somewhere. *Hep-Hep*, says Neil Diamond. *Hep-Hep – you want me. And I can't deny I'm a man.* The driver is looking at me through the rear-view mirror with his depressing, watery, blue-gray eyes.

'So you grew up abroad, didn't you?'

I don't answer.

'What's better? Here or there?'

I ignore the question and start cleaning my glasses with a used Kleenex. Ever since moving to Tehran, everyone from the plumber to the dentist to the janitor has been keen on hearing how I would personally compare Iran to the rest of the world. I put on my glasses again and reach for my packet of Super Golden Love Deluxe, a local brand with gold and lilac packaging, and light a cigarette, tossing the match out the window.

Owing to my parents' multinational careers in corporate pharmaceuticals, I grew up visiting various polyglot schools in Central and West African republics. After which I spent several years working part-time in cafés and sports bars in Oregon and Texas, which is where I met Stella, who persuaded me to move to the East Coast and study Hebrew and Arabic, along with a minor degree in Art History and a certificate in Criminal Forensics.

I came to Tehran for the first time just over a month ago. When questioned about motives for 'coming back', I refer to various lines of kinship, or my 'cherished mother tongue', and something about the light, the landscape, roots. The more I make myself sound like a palm tree, the more people are touched. It was of course Stella's idea that I move here in the first place.

The taxi heads down Revolution Avenue, towards Freedom Square. From the very start, I was struck by the fact that in central Tehran you're rarely more than twenty feet away from a pizzeria serving *chiizberger* in a setting of purple bathroom tiles, fake black marble and pink neon, with syrupy Iranian soft rock in the background.

But the city's appeal, I decide, as the taxi turns into the freeway leading to the Zirzamin housing estate, where both I and most of my acquaintances have studios or apartments, or both, must be the fact that Tehran doesn't try to please, consisting largely, as it does, of sand, dust, glass, neon and eight-lane motorways running straight through concrete housing projects. Surrounding the official city center are scores of satellite towns and villages that are very similar. Over the past twenty years or so, eight million locals have joined the preceding four, most of whom were newcomers themselves.

Swifter than speech, as I like to put it, somewhat theatrically. Lighter than language. To describe Tehran would be like spelling out a frenzied, hour-long quarrel over dinner to a newcomer at the table. Personally, I would take Tehran over Isfahan flower gardens and donkey bridges any day and find a smug sense of satisfaction in the fact that there are many who would beg to differ.

Very recently, European architects in Prada dinner jackets and Le Coq Sportif have been here, reciting statistics from Dutch coffee-table catalogues, of the new avant-garde status of Third-World metropoles carelessly breaking urban records, proportions, aesthetic standards. Western concepts and terminologies, they say, trying to sound apocalyptic, ominous, touched, enthusiastic and nonchalant at the same time, can no longer do justice to the many Tehrans of this shifting world.

I take out a small Moleskine notebook, 'a pocket format for everyday use, the same legendary notebook of Van Gogh and Matisse, of Hemingway and Chatwin', which is what I do after every situation, performance, exhibition, news programme or snippet of conversation I consider gainful for the Promessa in some way, specifying the date and place and archival epithet, Patronage, Bygones, Friends, Travel, Fashion, Administration, Hearsay, Opening or Closing. I prefer to give everything in my notebooks a narrative flow, a coherent storyline to frame and embed the material. This is more important than chronology or psychological realism. I've always hated loose ends, whether in essays, living-room scenographies, journals or notebooks. Be that as it may, most of what ends up in the notebooks is determined by Stella herself in the end, along lines and parameters she has never taken the time to spell out, and I've never insisted on knowing, preferring to see the whole thing as a private joke between the two of us, a modish play on fact and fiction and archival theories and the post-contemporary condition and such.

'You see, my little possum', I remember her telling me on the very day we met, in the teacherly, protective tone I was soon to cherish and look forward to, 'we can no longer set out to represent the historical past. We can only represent our ideas and stereotypes about that past. Is that something you can understand?'

I open the notebook to the last page, to a floor plan of the Revolutionary Courthouse on Shariati Street, then flick back to the beginning. 'The bourgeois artist now acts without clearly formulated reasons or intentions, which means that anything can become an indication of his authorial motivation, and that the whole planet has become one big collection of possible hints, clues and innuendos. Josef Stalin, 1944. Olympics 2000. Weightlifter Rezazadeh screws up fleshy, heinous face, lifting 1040 lbs. Olympic gold. Defeated favorite Ronny Weller: can't remember what he looks like, nor what his name is. Iranians are appearing out of nowhere. It's like being in a Spielberg. I slowly rip out the page and throw it out the window, then instantly regret having done so.

I can vaguely remember hitting on various women last night, none of whom showed any interest in me, not even after the cocaine. I can also recall House music remixes of early Madonna tracks that caused the neighbors to knock on the door around 4 AM, athough whether they were meaning to join in or complain I never found out.

The air flowing in through the open windows is cold and unpleasant. The driver takes a highway exit leading into the Zirzamin housing estate, an enormous assemblage of right angles, functional voids and horizontal strips of glass and concrete, the stuff people refer to as 'Stalinist', although Stalin, if I remember Stella's point correctly, actually preferred gigantic wedding-cake architecture, playful squiggles and pointed turrets. Designed in the mid-seventies, at the peak of the hysterical optimism of the Shah era, Zirzamin is said to be the largest housing estate in the Middle East. At an opening at the Ti-Tap gallery in north Tehran last week someone claimed it had more inhabitants than Sweden.

I immediately spot Mehrangiz sitting on a park bench in the outer courtyard of block 39A of the estate, not far from my own studio apartment in 44D. Mehrangiz watches the taxi approach, waiting for it to come to a complete halt before shutting her paperback and rearranging her headscarf and sunglasses. Only then does she stand up and head for the car. Mehrangiz is an up-and-coming video artist with a perfect gap between her front teeth. She's wearing olive green army pants, Charles Jourdan pumps and, by way of Islamic *hejab*, a Lonsdale scarf and an oversized Fred Perry polo shirt under her cashmere coat.

I watch her from the cab crossing the smooth concrete courtyard in the faint afternoon sunlight, realizing she is without question more attractive than Stella. Most people would find her plump, overweight even, but this doesn't bother me in the slightest. On the contrary. I appreciate the big cheeks and 'fuck me eyes', as Stella would put it, the women who differ from the average, proto-anorexic daddy's girl you see in north Tehran or thereabouts.

I try to relax the muscles in my gut by taking several deep breaths, as if to pull the air all the way down into my stomach. This is a technique I learned in acting classes as a teenager, for stage fright.

Mehrangiz climbs into the cab, smelling of some musky men's aftershave, and the driver and I both mumble a standard greeting before resuming the journey towards my grand-aunt Zsa Zsa's country estate in Karaj. I'm silently hoping Zsa Zsa will not embarrass me when we get to the farm, although presumably she will. With her corduroys, denim shirts and handsome, arrogant features, you might have seen a gentleman farmer in her, if it weren't for her high-pitched giggle and her pubescent sense of humor, despite being almost ninety years old. Zsa Zsa likes to surprise you by sticking her little finger in your ear and making obtrusive clicking and whistling sounds. Or by suggesting she recently had sex with one of your close relatives, out in her apple orchard somewhere.

Over the last fifty years or so, Zsa Zsa has earned the reputation of a skilled and distinguished hostess, clicks and whistles and other conversational gambits notwithstanding. She usually speaks very little and is considered an outstanding listener. During the many afternoons I've spent at her estate I've witnessed army officers, political dissidents, Kurdish Sufis, folk musicians, housewives, farmers, Swiss journalists, Arab tourists and a TV newscaster sitting on the veranda, mumbling to Zsa Zsa as she sits with her hands folded in her lap, head cocked to one side, doing a fantastic job of appearing to be sympathetic.

During the Iran-Iraq war, when Baghdad and Tehran were pelting each other with Soviet and American missiles, dozens of families moved out of the city center to stay at Zsa Zsa's. Long walks in the orchards, volleyball, date liquor, eleventh-century poetry. *The dust on your doorstep / a paradise to me / a fervent pheasant / I fling myself / on searing arrows of your glance.* Or suchlike. In the evening, there was cheap Goa technotrance, as remixed in LA or Istanbul, blasting from a tiny tape recorder. But also opium with sweet tea and sopping honey pastries.

As Mehrangiz and I arrive at the farm, we find a small group of visitors having a late lunch on the veranda. They all interrupt their meal to awkwardly stand up and shake hands. *Khoshbakhtam*

khoshbakhtam haleh shoma. In a confused fit of coquetry – compounded, indeed, by the enduring hangover – I decline to join them for lunch, looking on as Mehrangiz is offered cucumbers in yogurt with raisins and fresh mint, along with lamb and eggplant sauce on saffron rice, with sour berries and a baked crust.

Later, over black tea, honey pastries and pistachio-saffron ice cream, Mehrangiz praises me for the ideas I've been pursuing since my recent arrival, the showroom in the making, the many ingenious little plans for the Promessa website, the merchandising, the behind-the-scenes Promessa documentary.

'In Iran, such things are just so totally unexpected, so completely new to everyone. It's so much more appreciated than anywhere else.'

I nervously assume Mehrangiz is coming on to me, but then realize with disappointment that she isn't, so I snidely tell her that to impress the locals with flashy gadgets and cosmopolitan prattle, I could just as well move to Wimbledon, but then stop, seeing as she's not really listening. She smiles at me, rubs my elbow absent-mindedly and goes and sits down next to Zsa Zsa at the other end of the veranda. I light a cigarette and watch them chat as they carefully sip their hot black tea from small, gold-rimmed glasses.

Like most of the art scene here, I'm not exactly of proletarian ancestry myself, what with the family owning the small town of Ozgalabad in its entirety, only two hours northeast of Tehran. In the late twenties all of my paternal great-grandfathers and great-granduncles were officers under Reza Shah. Reza was the Iranian Atatürk, keen on modernizing the country by any means necessary. Iran, he insisted, was to be taken seriously. Reza found the term 'Persia' embarrassing – it smacked of water pipes and flying carpets – and had it replaced by 'Iran', which refers to the country's Aryan heritage.

According to Stella, the Aryans were little more than a despairing mob of hungry Siberians who had settled in what is now Iran a very long time ago. Most had long forgotten they had ever existed, when a small flock of German Romantics in wigs, white stockings and puffy shirtsleeves suddenly decided the Aryans had successfully colonized vast parts of Asia and Greece and declared them the 'Cradle of Civilization'. Apparently, Reza Shah very much approved, as do many Iranians nowadays.

Reza, in any case, found nomadic tribes at least as embarrassing as water pipes, if not more so, and took to luring the tribal leaders to peace talks or religious ceremonies, where he had them imprisoned or shot. This was the line of work my ancestors were in, before settling down in what was still a village a good stretch away from Tehran. Here, the family proceeded, rather typically for military stock, to bully, threaten and buy out the locals until they finally owned the village as a whole.

Unlike my father's side of the family – very *Blut-und-Boden*, very happily belligerent – my mother's was more affected and self-conscious but just as blessed, if not more so, with government connections, a healthy sense of opportunism and a more or less feudal standing, at one point even running a private railway on their estate. The family fortune was closely related to Shell discovering oil on the property in the early twentieth century. At this point, the only child, Zsa Zsa, had barely learned to walk, talk and ride horseback, when it was already decided that she was to learn four languages and study six more, including Latin, Greek, Aramaic and Sanskrit.

To this day, I do not know where precisely this piece of land might lie. In an interview with *Paris Match*, Zsa Zsa mentions Surkhana in east Azerbaijan. Various aunts and uncles, however, insist it wasn't Azerbaijan at all, but somewhere in Georgian Abkhazia. I sincerely suspect they may be purposely misleading me, for reasons I cannot know. Stella has offered to contact friends in Baku who'd help find and perhaps even retrieve the estate, with the help of her own family lawyers if needs be. But I assume this would irretrievably place the land, and the resulting perks of all possible kinds, at the service of Stella and her many little schemes, networks and joint ventures, and am not quite convinced by her suggestion. At least not yet.

Be that as it may, one crisp November morning in 1917 the entire family leaves discreetly for France. Paris in the twenties is a confusing place, and the family soon blows everything it has on social clubs, fashion and cocaine. On 25 November 1941 Zsa Zsa becomes the third woman to join the French Foreign Legion and, over the next twenty years or so, she has a dazzling career as a driver and explosives operator in Algeria and Indochina, during which she loses half a lung, a part of her liver and four ribs, along with any sense of respect for human life, though she does win a *Croix de Chevalier de la Légion d'Honneur* and an interview in *Paris Match*.

In the early sixties Zsa Zsa moves to Tehran to open the Promessa on what was then Palace Street, on the corner of Queen Elizabeth Boulevard, now renamed Palestine Street, on the corner of Farmer Avenue. Even in her sixties Zsa Zsa liked to spend most of her time entertaining her guests by the bar, or guepard hunting in southern Iran, or taking long evening walks with her nieces, including my mother. Every last Wednesday of the month she would buy them dozens of tiny wooden cages stuffed with disfigured, undernourished sparrows, so the girls could send them flying off into the sunset. The nieces all agree to become lawyers when they grow up.

Zsa Zsa also spends many an afternoon with friends from the SAVAK secret service. Together they sip Turkish coffee in her office, listening to Beatles and Bob Dylan tracks on her tape recorder. *The pump don't work cause the vandals took the handles.* In the meantime, many other friends and acquaintances of Zsa Zsa's – mostly smugglers, Maoists, Leninists, Trotskyists, Stalinists, 'Third Way' Communists, Social Democrats or Islamic Socialists – patiently hide from the SAVAK officers in the cellars of the Promessa. They smoke black-market cigarettes and struggle to keep their voices down as they debate the role and relevance of the Soviet vanguard within Iran, or bitterly accuse each other of countless forms of collusion and collaboration with all sorts of enemies within and without, the soothing sounds of the tape spools occasionally wafting down from the office above their heads. *Sergeant Pepper's Lonely Sergeant Pepper's Lonely Sergeant Pepper's Lonely Sergeant Pepper's Lonely Sergeant Pepper's Lonely Hearts Club band.*

Stella tells me my colorful background – armed violence and *dolce farniente* – is exactly what she looks for in a friend and, especially, she adds warmly, in a colleague. She makes me tell the anecdotes over and over, demanding more and more details, sometimes expressing angry disappointment over facts revealed.

'The desk was walnut? Walnut? Oh my God, walnut. OK, never mind.'

I've long realized these are the only occasions I'd ever see Stella moved by anything other than her own professional ambitions.

From its very opening night, the Promessa is frequented by Russian and Georgian exiles, disco glitterati, modish members of the gauche caviar, including the occasional Maoists, Neo-Leninists, Trotskyists, 'Third Way' Communists, Post-Stalinists and the odd Social Democrat; but also US Vice-president Spiro Agnew, the Shah and his Queen, the delightful ex-Queen Soraya and her alternating lovers, and Errol Garner, who indulges in an *amour fou* with Zsa Zsa. Rock Hudson is said to have very much enjoyed the onion blinis with sour cream and once tipped the waiter with an imitation gold Rolex. Freddy Mercury's parents, the Bulsaras, are rumored to have met at the bar over Kir Royales and honey-roasted peanuts.

Late in the evenings, Zsa Zsa and her chums take to singing rueful Georgian gypsy songs, and together they cry and moan until they can't lift their heads from the table anymore, so the microphone is propped up between two glasses and nudged into Zsa Zsa's face while she sings and slobbers on the tablecloth.

Every once in a while the Shah insists on having the entire salon to himself. Simon, *chef de cuisine*, is obliged personally to taste the exclusively prepared appetizers in the presence of SAVAK officers. After his visits, the *shah-n-shah-e-aryamehr*, King of Kings of Aryan Virtue, a gentleman whose tie-pin collection costs more than Belgium, habitually leaves without paying.

His spouse, Queen Farah, on the other hand, prefers to have

an aperitif among her subjects and appears incognito, in a gigantic pair of Christian Dior shades. But the SAVAK invariably secure the premises before she arrives, and the only subjects present are strategically seated agents and the family relatives themselves, obliged to pose as customers, politely enquiring about the *vin du jour*. This was pre-revolutionary Tehran, before things took a turn, not necessarily for the worse, in many ways indeed for the better.

The hangover is finally subsiding. Zsa Zsa's swimming pool lies in the shade of an enormous oak tree, from which an occasional leaf or twig plummets down into the cool, dark water. Two men with shaved chests, gold chains and perfect tans are floating around on inflatable mattresses shaped into oversized cellphones. Visibly bored, they collect the twigs and stick them between their toes. A pop diva from Uzbekistan makes pleasant cooing noises from within the tape deck.

During the course of the evening, as the air cools down and mosquitoes and cicadas make their appearance, a drunken discussion on politics unfolds, reformism pitted against conspiracy, reformism as conspiracy, conspiracies *tout court*. Mehrangiz categorically stands up for the Iranian cause, the exemplary character of the Iranian model, the dignity of the Iranian people and the maturity of the Iranian masses, getting caught up in contradicting moral platitudes, until she finally falls quiet, staring down at her Charles Jourdan, sporting a furious expression on her peachy face.

Recently, in an uptown Hare Krishna restaurant, I watched Mehrangiz scream at a helpless waiter, a slender young man in fashionable spectacles and a dark orange T-shirt, for a period of almost four minutes.

'A reservation? A reservation. Listen. Listen to me, darling. I'm *not having any* of your *fascist* propaganda.'

The restaurant fell silent, except for the waiter's faltering apologies and George Harrison on the hi-fi. *Goooh – vinn – daaa*, said George Harrison.

Later, I can see Zsa Zsa standing by the garden gate, her ivory walking cane in hand, talking to five young men surrounding a small, bearded figure in a traditional kaftan frock. Having now given up trying to catch Mehrangiz's attention, I walk over to Zsa Zsa, who introduces me to her 'new neighbor', who turns out to be the famous revolutionary clergyman Tarofi himself.

In the years following the revolution, Tarofi was a notorious political figure, a cleric, traveling judge and henchman in one. Along with other supporters of the budding Islamic Republic, Tarofi took it upon himself to rid the fledgling state of its enemies in an uncomplicated, down-to-earth manner. I recently learned that these enemies of the state – mostly the very Maoists, Neo-Leninists, Trotskyists, Post-Stalinists, Social Democrats, 'Third Way' Communists or Islamic Socialists who mingled in Zsa Zsa's cellar and, later, at the Promessa – were betrayed by their own comrades, desperate to save their necks.

At the time, one of Zsa Zsa's closest drinking buddies was an emphatic Trotskyist, who annoyingly insisted on calling himself Leo and who would sit on Zsa Zsa's patio reciting early Soviet poetry, Supremacist machismo in delicate verse, duly translated into Farsi. One summer afternoon, Tarofi paid Leo a brief visit and dealt him a shot to the head in his own backyard.

These days, Tarofi is known to wear the same pair of vintage Kojak sunglasses at all times. His beard is remarkably thick, wooly and amorphous. For security reasons, he is continuously accompanied by his many sons. Tarofi insists on speaking English. He sounds a lot like Joe Cocker.

'Europe: very good nice. Very nice, very good,' he croaks. 'Learn English in Birmingham.'

'Birmingham. So you've been to England.'

'Yes. Switzerland for gun.'

'Gun.'

'Yes. Switzerland. Engineers ABB. Brown Bovering.'

'Guns for who?'

'Guns for Iran. Very good nice.'

'Yes. So you've been to Switzerland. Zurich or Geneva?'

'Go Bern.' He hesitates, smoothes his beard and adds, 'You know Stella.'

I feign mild *ennui*. 'Yes. Yes, I do know Stella.'

'And Mr Badbakht? Have you met Mr Badbakht?'

'I don't believe I have.'

So we chat, in Farsi now, and all of a sudden Tarofi doesn't sound half as imbecilic as he does in English, and I'm actually a little shocked to find him perfectly sharp and articulate. I eventually venture something like, 'Mr Tarofi must have many anecdotes to tell about his exploits in the name of the revolution, he put in such great effort, may God give him life,' and other standard platitudes, but Tarofi refuses to go there.

'We've made mistakes, as everyone very well knows. What do you expect me to say? We believed in what we were doing.

But things have changed. And so have we. Just be grateful for the mercy of a tardy birth, my friend. Do not judge history. Be grateful, that's all.'

According to popular legend, after the victorious World Cup soccer game against the US some years ago, Tarofi saw dancing couples and unveiled womanfolk on the street and wished to express his approval. 'I share your happiness,' he grunted at them. When the dancers recognized him, they formed a circle around Tarofi, clapping their hands and jeering, 'Hajji's gotta dance, Hajji's gotta dance.' Tarofi, confused and disappointed, returned home to his many sons. Now, he turns back to Zsa Zsa, asks her a long list of questions on irrigation techniques – getting so expensive, how *are* we supposed to manage, I remember when a precision spraying pump was half, no, a third of the price, and do you have any idea where I can get those German pruning scissors, simply the best – then waddles quickly off into the Karaj twilight, his sons scrambling after him like keyed-up groupies.

On the way home from Zsa Zsa's, the taxi follows the Alborz mountains until it reaches the Hausmannian boulevards of west Tehran. It's three in the morning, and the radio is playing a keyboard version of '*El Bodeguero*'. The landscape is punctuated by small concrete sheds and brightly colored neons of pink and green.

As we approach Zirzamin, I look up to my apartment, fourth from the right on the twentieth floor, and I am, as always, relieved to see the lights are switched off. Ever since moving here, I cannot shake the fascinating, compulsive fear of arriving home one night to realize someone has been, or still is, inside the apartment.

Since first hearing of Zirzamin, only months ago, I'm amazed to find it evolving into a playground not only for international architects in Le Coq Sportif but also for budding political scientists and their doctoral theses. What we have here, they like to say, trying to sound apocalyptic, enthusiastic and nonchalant at the same time, is a remarkable example of the urbanization of consciousness in Iran and the re-inscription of the concept of a modern civil society as we know it. Note that in Zirzamin, inhabitants from completely different backgrounds, rather than live in separate parts of town, share a single space and are actually forced to get along. Gradually, a common discursive practice emerges, you see, that does not bear itself as a grand narrative, but sets itself apart from the *grands discours* of both High Modernism and the Islamic Republic.

That's if they're the Anglo-American, cultural-studies types, with light brown Manhattan Portage backpacks. If they're French, they walk around making diagrams and surveys on Heroin and Unemployment in the Ghetto Wastelands of west Tehran, *C'est vraiment le Bronx,* then publish it in the *Monde Diplomatique*, with an illustration by Edvard Munch. I am seized, captured by an overwhelming notion of lyrical acumen, gushing prose, seductive and smooth. But already sensing that, when the taxi stops in front of my block, I'll be finding myself staring blankly at a motionless 0.4 mm Staedtler rollerball in my hand, I leave the notebook unopened in my inside pocket.

I wonder whether I shouldn't move the gallery showroom to Zirzamin, Zsa Zsa the *genius loci* notwithstanding. Of course house and ghost went together, and of course it's always thrilling to witness past dreams and nightmares weighing on the living.

But nothing compares to the exquisitely fascist thrust of what I see through the cab window before me. Not even a zebra-striped anal passage figuring as an entrance. Zirzamin, I muse, dreamily reaching, after all, for my notebook, may well be the perfect allegory for anything I could possibly think of saying on Tehran, Iran or suchlike.

The idea, of course, is pointless. *Genius loci* aside, I agreed on everything with Stella long before, down to the very last detail, so it's a little too late to change my mind. There are only eight weeks left until the opening, and Stella isn't one for surprises, to say the least. Nothing that isn't planned to mind-numbing perfection, from the content of the notebooks to afternoon tea at Tarofi's.

Bygones

In my early teens, I lived with my parents in downtown Lagos, in a small and inconspicuous modern villa by the Ikoyi lagoon. One evening, just after my fourteenth birthday, my parents throw a welcome dinner for the new cultural attaché of the Austrian embassy. My mother spends most of the afternoon with the kitchen help, preparing the entrées. Cocktail egg-glazed vol-au-vents with oyster mushrooms, Peri-Peri vegetable choux puffs with chilli prawn salsa. The kitchen help is an agricultural science student from Ghana. Before taking a seat at the head of table, she takes great care to explain how to decorate the main course, pig roast. 'Don't forget to put parsley in the nose,' she tells her kitchen helper.

Most of the guests are West German and Austrian diplomats sipping on gin tonics, dressed in multihued ethnic garments, their wives in white linen shirts and discreet tribal necklaces. Along the walls are Yoruba masks of massive, black wood, tastefully arranged. Sitting to one side of the table is our family friend and nextdoor neighbor, Tan Christenhuber, who is to introduce me to Stella some ten years later. Seated next to him is a Swiss-German businessman from Basel with generous sweat patches up and down his back. The conversation takes a relaxed and familiar course: Paul Simon's *Graceland* LP, the ever-pending military coup – would do the country some good, you know, a stronger hand to guide it along – the new edition of short stories by Heinrich Böll, malaria prevention. So I heard primaquine makes you blind you mean chloroquine oh yes chloroquine exactly well I gave mine to the steward I mean they are more robust than us you know. They've been through a lot I can tell you.

When the door finally swings open, the kitchen help is standing in the doorway with generous bundles of parsley shoved up his nose and a pig roast on a silver platter.

'Fabulous!' shouts the Swiss-German, and a drop of red wine trickles out of his left nostril as he giggles and splutters into a napkin.

The blinds in my Zirzamin studio apartment are usually rolled down, admitting only cinematic, piercing shards of sunlight. The room is almost always empty save for a 1964 Corbusier sofa, a matching armchair, a portable Sony 220R and a *Rebutia Aureispina* cactus. A stack of olive-green notebooks forms a small pile under the armchair, next to which is a coffee table piled with several vintage ashtrays and fashion and design magazines, and printouts of several recent emails from Stella.

Pinned to the wall of my studio, just above the coffee table, is a large medallion, a cast bronze plaque with 'Indochine' inscribed above the silhouettes of three elephants – a gift from Zsa Zsa – and a Polaroid snapshot of Stella in a turquoise turtleneck and a satin paisley headscarf. Beneath the photograph is a frumpish, tacky postcard of Ho Chi Minh, waving happily at the camera with a senile grin on his face.

I turn on the Sony portable, switching to CNN for a habitual audio backdrop of jingles, headline fanfares and the subtle accents of globalized newscasters with Nescafé complexions and quirky surnames. For varying acoustic ambience, I at times resort to the BBC, Al-Jazeera, MTV Asia or East European soft porn channels, although this is now rare. I fear I may sooner or later give in to those alluring scenes of physical indulgence in Romanian pine forests and sparse Bulgarian bedrooms. The risk of one day catching myself in front of the screen with a box of Kleenex is a possibility I find humiliating and rather terrible.

I pour myself a scotch and add a shot of pomegranate juice, then switch over to the BBC. The newscaster is commenting on a press conference in Sacramento, a wry and unmistakable touch of irony in his voice. At the conference, an elderly Japanese-American is speaking to a cluster of amused journalists, most of them giggling, smiling and whispering to each other. The Japanese-American in question is a Hollywood tattoo artist awaiting trial for tattooing Japanese curses and obscenities on his unknowing customers, many of them celebrities. His scheme was exposed during Marilyn Manson's *Tainted Japan* tour, when the local press commented on the tattoo around Manson's navel, saying 'Please Insert General Wu's Chicken Here'.

The tattoo artist looks relaxed, even pleased with himself. A simple act of retribution, he says, matter-of-factly, for his clients' 'ignorance and arrogance' towards the ethnic import of what was decorating their arms and shoulders, backs and buttocks.

I switch the Sony portable back to CNN, then to Balkan Bang for a glimpse of anal sex in a horse-drawn wagon in the old part of Prague, before turning off the set. When I try to reach Mehrangiz, who stayed on at Zsa Zsa's last night, her cellphone is switched off. I light another Super Love Lights Deluxe, then turn the Sony back on.

TF1 is interviewing Uncle Tan, or Dr Christenhuber, rather, who is presented as an *'expert en matière de terrorisme'*. Tan is wearing a peculiar felt hat on his large, conic head. There's something intriguing about the way he cranes his long neck, staring at the ceiling with droopy eyelids, then suddenly jabs his impeccably manicured fingers to the rhythm of what he's saying.

'This way,' he purrs, 'the terrorist turns the whole world into a realm of signs, anything can be an indication of their presence, but also, anything, any snippet of text, or any bomb scare, can be a coded message for their own network, or a camouflage operation, a calculated distraction.'

Somehow, despite the dogged, virile air about him, Christenhuber's eyelids make him look as if he's always fighting an urge to fall asleep out of sheer disinterest.

'But you see, the Twin Tower affair notwithstanding, they're now running the risk of repetition. Of becoming a gimmick. Which is why I say they're bound to come up with something new any moment now. Something unprecedented in ambiguity and mystery and, and, well, in visual intelligence and entertainment value and so on.'

I switch off the TV set, light another cigarette and mix myself a homemade grape vodka, with crushed ice and a touch of lemon.

How is everything? Still in Russia. Getting things done. Someone said Cantonese is now officially the second language of St Petersburg, and I'm immensely attached to this fact, not because of what it means, but because it is the only thing I've managed to remember lately. Went to see this Vuillard exhibition at the Royal Academy, and I definitely favor the zero-psychology style of a portrait painter who just has someone reading a paper or dealing with things, and not demanding to be *read* by the viewer, which is reassuring. Like all the Russians here in St Petersburg – just wearing mink and getting on with it. But whether I do or do not make it to Tehran, you will have the kitsch Tehran Flower cacophony on Shariati to attend to please. After which most certainly you will have the interrogations, the threats, possibly beatings or worse and the Montana Lights. Remember they remove the filter. Oh and a big 'salaam' to Tarofi. Must rush (patent exaggeration, but, you know, 'at work'). Yours, Stella

I wake up towards noon, and take a walk to the corner store on the corner of blocks 44D and 44E, to buy a fresh pack of cigarettes and a new flask of *Gol-e Khalkhali* mouth spray. Early in the morning, the store is invariably filled with construction workers standing around drinking ice-cold chocolate milk in tiny glass bottles, but this time of day the shop is empty. I have a bottle of cold chocolate milk and talk soccer with the shopkeeper, and I'm just about to leave when a strictly veiled woman walks in.

She has the classic, almond-shaped bulging eyes you see in the miniature paintings, along with healthy cheekbones, a nose-job and ruthlessly plucked eyebrows, down to a minuscule, graceful sliver of dark stubble. I tightly clutch my bottle, pulling the air deep into my gut, watching from the corner of my eye as she orders a packet of Golden Love Deluxe Lights, a family pack of Wrigley's Spearmint, biodegradable Tampax Slender Regular, transparent Scotch tape and two 80-watt light bulbs.

While the clerk is adding up the bill on his solar-powered calculator, she suddenly turns towards me, opens her veil and lifts it up above her head with her arms outstretched. After holding it there for perhaps half a second or less, she rearranges the fabric with small, quick movements of her hands, then pulls it down tightly again, straightening the veil by yanking it firmly against the back of her head, before flapping it around herself once again. A flurry of shimmering black folds reflects the neon light from the ceiling. For this brief span of time, lasting no longer than four seconds, the blank expression on her face doesn't change. I cannot even tell whether she's noticed me standing there in front of her. It's only now I realize she's been talking soccer with the shopkeeper all along. No Stuttgart VFB they'll never get anywhere but Werder Bremen they seem to have a few tricks up their sleeve what's with that new midfielder what's his name.

I follow her out of the store, walking only ten feet behind her as she moves towards blocks 39 and 38, but I give up when I see her enter the *Vafa* fitness center, where today, like every other Sunday, Tuesday, and Thursday, is women only day.

This evening, I'm invited to a wedding party in south Tehran. I do not know the bride, nor the groom, so I'm grateful to my friend, the sculptor Cyrus Rahati, for taking me along. The party is certain to be different to the inebriated, trashy disco nights that apparently pass for wedding celebrations up north.

Chaotic as Tehran may be, if you consider its division between north and south, *balaye shahr* and *paine shahr*, which marks the partition between the haves and have-nots, the city is very organized, even quaint. One is generally liable to size people up not only by their neighborhood wedding ceremonies but by the way they sip their tea or pluck their eyebrows. It can be worse than London. Even Munich.

Cyrus's neighborhood, where the party is held, is further south than the main station, deep within the darkest depths of working-class neighborhoods. So decidedly *paine shahr*, I've never been able to see it as anything more than an abstract blur at the bottom of my city map. This is where, as Cyrus is always happy to point out, 'chi-chi gallerists' do not particularly like to set foot, unless they're presenting Historical Tehran to nervous tourists.

Cyrus was once a *bassiji* militant after the revolution, then a foot soldier in the war against Iraq, after which he returned to Tehran to earn a living as a watermelon and grapefruit vendor. This was when Cyrus taught himself how to sculpt, in the back of his fruit stand after closing shop in the evenings, later enrolling at an art academy and now actually enjoying the frills and the media attention of a budding career on the international art market. Behold the south Tehran modernist, said the BBC, trying to sound apocalyptic, enthusiastic and nonchalant at the same time.

I meet Cyrus at the train station, where we share a motorbike cab to the wedding hall. From outside, the ballroom is marked by a shop window full of voguish bouquets of artificial flowers and neon lights spelling 'Hall of Mirrors', in searing orange. We go up two flights of stairs and reach a corridor, which is where we

34

take a left, into the men's section, an enormous room awash with stark neon light, filled with rows of men, chewing on cucumbers and tangerines. In the spirit of public decency, the excesses of the bachelor party are hidden from the women's section by a wall reaching almost to the ceiling.

Having arrived with Cyrus, a man of credibility well acquainted with nearly every guest in the room, I follow him up and down countless rows of men and boys, shaking hands and smiling what I hope is a likable, thoughtful sort of smile that doesn't look too apologetic. *Khoshbakhtam khoshbakhtam.* Beaming an especially likable, thoughtful, apologetic sort of smile whenever I'm introduced as a gentleman who has just arrived from abroad.

I take a seat and, doing as everyone does, first have a cucumber, then go for the tangerines. I feel alienated from the men around me. After a lifetime of telling Americans and heavily perspiring Swiss expats I was Iranian in a self-important and stubborn sort of way, I find myself feeling oddly xenophobic. I succeed in starting a conversation with Cyrus's second cousin, who turns out to be writing a thesis on 'The Backgammon Motif in Postmodern Persian Literature' and begin to feel a little better. Most of the men are still peacefully staring at their napkins.

Later on in the evening, the lettered second cousin starts explaining his fondness for the Beats. As he elaborates on the 'widely misread relationship between Dean Moriarty and Kerouac' I reach for an apple, then change my mind and have another tangerine. From the women's section, I can hear the happy sounds of people shouting, clapping and leaping up and down. 'So by the time he finally gets to Tangiers, where he meets up with Burroughs and Ginsberg and everything, Kerouac is totally burnt out. He's totally fucked up.'

When the designated entertainer takes to the stage the men hardly blink. The entertainer is the type of middle-aged Iranian who looks very much like Al Pacino. Slow, deliberate movements, sad, drooping eyes and arched eyebrows that convey a permanent expression of disbelief. He goes into a long spiel on the religious status of clapping. 'I know there's a *looooota* mullahs out there in the audience tonight', he croons, 'and we know they *reeeeally* don't like the idea of clapping.' He begins a long chain of anecdotes, cracks and proverbs on the theological status of applause.

'So let's give the newlyweds a hand,' he coyly concludes. People chuckle, put down their cucumbers and clap. By now the shrieking, stomping, whooping and clapping from the women's section is all but deafening, and it's hard to understand what the man is saying.

He starts telling jokes. A plane crash-lands on a cannibal island. Papa cannibal and his son are watching the passengers stumble out of the aircraft. 'Let's eat that woman!' says the son. 'No, son, she's too scrawny,' says Papa Cannibal. 'Then let's eat that guy!' 'No, son, he's too fat, it's not good for you, imagine the cholesterol.' Finally, this young, bad *hejab* woman comes out of the plane. Her headscarf is pulled back *waaaay* over here, she's got makeup, short skirt, high heels, no socks, you get the picture. 'Let's eat her!' says the son. 'Don't be stupid,' says the father, 'We'll eat your mother instead!'

The men giggle, yawn or play with their toothpicks. Pacino launches into song. He has a good voice and goes through religious songs, folk songs, male bonding songs. One is a slow hymn to the women of Iran. If you want a woman who's pretty and sweet, gooo to Shiraaaz – If you want a woman who's funny and cheerful, gooo to Abadaaan – If you want a woman who's smart and strong, gooo to Tabriiiiiz – but remember, gentlemen, remember it takes money, it takes a car, it takes a house. And so on.

The groom finally arrives, looking utterly exhausted, and everyone stands and applauds as he's surrounded by digital hi-8 video cameras and big clouds of cash that people throw at him as he passes, hordes of little boys squabbling over the money as it floats to the ground. As he walks around the ballroom, shaking hands and smiling politely, the kids stumble around him, kicking over chairs and glasses and sending fruit and cutlery flying through the room as they fight over the cash.

He finally makes it to the stage, where he takes a seat between two young men in suits, his *saqdush*. Strictly speaking, the lettered second cousin explains, a *saqdush* is a 'good-looking, experienced young man who stands by the groom during his wedding' and offers him advice, particularly when it comes to what, supposedly, only married men have been through before. In practice, the *saqdush* is merely expected to sit beside the groom and look pretty for a little while. Piled up before them on silver platters are handsome, pyramidal architectures of tangerines, oranges and cucumbers.

Pacino is bursting into song once again, when there's a whiff of food in the air, and everyone scrambles to their feet, throws themselves at the meat sauce and the rice cakes, eats as quickly as they possibly can and leaves immediately, to wait for their sisters, mothers, wives and girlfriends in the searing orange neon light outside the door.

At an opening at the uptown Shahrzad art gallery the next day, I was surprised to walk into Tarofi, still surrounded by his many sons. Art and paint. Very good nice.

Though I try to keep my distance, Tarofi lays a chummy arm around my shoulder and tells me of a Rotterdam Conference honoring the 'Planetary Peace Prize for People's Rights', where he has been invited to speak as a 'voice of reformism in the Islamic world', very good, very nice, then croakingly introduces me to an illustrious abstract painter who has spent the past two decades teaching his own work to students of the various Tehran art academies: sixties op-art with meaningful admixtures of lyrical, folkloric touches.

I chuckle at the professor's jokes, compliment his wife on her Chanel headscarf and even offer the professor a solo exhibit at the Promessa, complete with a lecture series on retinal exhaustion, along with an all-night reading of the key texts of Gestalt Psychology, then move away, intending to leave as soon as I possibly can.

I've already reached the exit, lighting a cigarette and checking my watch as I walk, when I remember Stella's email and thus have to make my way back through the blur of nose-jobs, platitudes and eau de cologne, to give Tarofi Stella's regards. Predictably, he lightens up and insists what a shame it is I am leaving so early and couldn't we have coffee the next day or the day after, reminding me he has only just acquired an apartment in Zirzamin, block 70 or thereabouts, in one of the slabs a touch more brutalist than those of Franco-Iranian make, perhaps because they were built by Korean engineers at a later date. Oh so you've never seen the Korean ones from within, well that's a shame. I mean isn't it great we're neighbors now, we could get to know each other a little better, now wouldn't that be something – see, I've only just just moved there, and already I get a letter from the tenant's association saying how proud they are to have me, believe me, they were so sweet.

If, at least to Stella's mind, there are common denominators in Iran which cut through profession, religion, class and gender – classical poetry, Aryanism or any type of junk food soaked in sweet ketchup – even these are subject to styles and modes of consumption that differ. One of the few phenomena that truly unite the proud people of Persia as a whole is the fascination for paw-foot rococo armchairs with baroque crimson paddings and gold trimmings, shaped into teeny-tiny crests and curls, leaves and feathers. In Tehran, more is more, and every other apartment is a painstakingly arranged baroque furniture showroom, full of flamboyant loops and adorable little curves, a cross between Ziggy Stardust and Louis XV. At times, as in the case of the Tarofi duplex, the sofa still sports the original plastic wrapping.

On Tarofi's coffee table is a small, ceramic canoe filled with porcelain apples, peaches and pears. Sipping my Earl Grey tea, I admire the ormolu chandelier, fringed curtains and framed reproduction of an oil painting of a Dutch peasant woman in clogs and a peaked white hat.

Tarofi is chuckling to himself and wagging his hands about in small flapping motions. He has taken off his sunglasses and turban and placed them beside him on the plastic wrapping of the sofa. Although Tarofi's eyes are sagging and bloodshot, like some gigantic cocker spaniel's, he seems more relaxed and more cheerful than usual. His sons are nowhere to be seen; perhaps that had something to do with it.

'You'll find quite a few contradictions between private Gestalt and public design in Tehran.' He chuckles.

I nod, but I've seen the apartment and would like to leave, its build being little more interesting or noteworthy than those in 44D. The rooms too small, the corridors awkward. The Zirzamin project certainly has its majestic, brutal, uncompromising splendor from without, but once inside, it is at best the furniture that leaves a lasting impression.

'See, the Islamic revolution was clearly a postmodern gesture, and so a project such as Zirzamin would be out of place here. But clearly the advantage of big, monumental projects, whether they're revolutions or books or buildings', he pauses and leans forward, speaking quickly and quietly, almost in a whisper, 'is that, if you have the right proportions, you can adapt from within. Silently, discreetly. From post to neo – and back.' Even though Tarofi clearly isn't the moron he appeared to be at first glance, I hadn't expected him to be as stilted and highbrow in his architectural positions.

'Corbusier no good nice,' he adds, in his customary baby English, before continuing in solemn, grandfatherly Mullah Farsi. 'This is clearly the kind of thing people like you and I should be thinking about. You know the rumor about Zirzamin being one big calligraphic homage to the Shah? That it spells out "Long Live the Shah" if you look down from above? I smile nervously, close my notebook, open it again and pretend to take notes.

'Writing, you see, is just as monumental as architecture. Why is this? Because it generates the truth in history, the truth in the

40

family name. Architecture does not depend on construction sites, but on the knowledge of approved principles. On the authority to build on them. Take Alexander's Persian porch. What do we find here? All these majestic columns, each one a Persian soldier supporting the edifice.'

I'm reminded of Mehrangiz, who I'm meeting later on today and who lives nearby. We've agreed to drive around the city in her Honda Civic this evening, to see the streetlights marking the twenty-second anniversary of the revolution and perhaps document them on video. Every year, the whole of Tehran, north and south, is filled with blinking neon butterflies in pink and yellow, neon swans in purple and green, neon flowers in blue and orange, and climactic government slogans in bright red.

I briefly speculate on her taste in living-room furniture but soon find myself rehearsing fantasies involving her generous bust, along with her ankles and the small of her back, as well as her broad shoulders and Germanic cheekbones. The idea of dropping by on a surprise visit makes me enjoyably nervous and uneasy.

'But no one thinks Zirzamin is monumental or imperial or anything.' I shut my notebook again. 'No one. It'll go down as a breeding ground for crack dealers and teenage suicides. Even *France Info* did a story on teenagers throwing themselves off the rooftops of Zirzamin. You think you have to watch your head when you turn a corner.'

'Yes. But that only makes it even more, more hyper-monumental.' Tarofi is waving his hands about again, but dismissively and impatiently. He sighs and smiles at me in a resigned, tired sort of way. I now notice Tarofi's quirky side parting, reminiscent of the distinct style of a French soccer legend whose name I cannot quite put my finger on.

'Take any traditional part of town. Even if hundreds of pubescent kids chuck themselves out of their bedroom windows on one and the same morning, nobody will say it's because of the traditional neighborhood, because of little brick courtyards with little goldfish wiggling about in little garden ponds. Whereas in Zirzamin, you will find more human tragedies attached to the name. Why is this? Because of a hundred thousand people inscribing a single space.' Platini, I now remember. Tarofi's side parting is exactly the same as Michel Platini's.

Despite Tarofi's acquaintance with Stella and his ruminations on the ways of leaving a violent, unmistakable mark in human history, which Stella would indeed have appreciated, I'm bored to sheer nausea. I noisily finish my glass of tea and look up at my host expectingly, waiting for him to stand up and walk over to the kitchen samovar for a fresh kettle, then quietly get up and leave, leaving the door open behind me. I hurry down the stairs to the ground floor, and it is only in the courtyard that I remember that Tarofi really is not the kind of man you would want to aggravate or provoke, but the Mullah's postmodern palaver and his natty taste in living-room furniture has somehow rendered him approachable and sweet, even human, in a way. I decide to make it up to Tarofi some other day and start walking towards Mehrangiz's block, breathing deeply, but reconsider the idea of a surprise visit and walk back home.

Barely two hours after sipping Early Grey with Tarofi I'm driving down Enqelab Avenue in Mehrangiz's Honda, listening to her drone on contentedly about her latest video project, called

'Twenty', a fictional piece set in duplex apartments in postmodern skyscrapers in north Tehran. The storyline, or topic, if I understand correctly, is that of a love triangle between two affluent single mothers and an Afghani kitchen help. At some point, the Afghani blows up the Azadi monument with a makeshift bomb, just as the single mothers are sentenced to death by stoning, by a judge played by Jeff Koons in a cameo appearance.

According to the latest version of Mehrangiz's script, the kitchen help lives in the hollow steel pedestal of an enormous advertising billboard for Nokia cellphones. I know for a fact that hundreds of Afghanis – the lowest-priced and hardest-working labor you can find in Tehran – do indeed dwell in billboard contraptions of the kind, but I consider the story a scam nonetheless. With Tehran one of the flattest metropoles worldwide, setting a vaguely dissenting movie in ostentatious high-rises would amount to little more than a cheap rip-off. A rather typical ploy to earn a pat on the back as the daring, dissident filmmaker, holding moving talks for understanding audiences in progressive European venues with Frida Kahlo retrospectives and glossy catalogues.

So I smile at Mehrangiz and make sarcastic, unfair remarks on bourgeois radicalism, even though I find her suggestion I play the Afghani kitchen boy myself tremendously flattering, even tempting, a unique opportunity to finally put my teenage acting classes to better use. That aside, working side by side with Mehrangiz, I realize, would in many ways be a tactical opportunity, a strategic advantage.

As she takes a left into Shariati Avenue, precisely as I was expecting her to, since Shariati is even more vividly decked with screaming neon than any other boulevard in the city, we pass a telegenic flower stand with a big and beguiling sign, TEHRAN FLOWER in flashing orange. Mehrangiz obligingly parks by the side of the road, walks around the car to the trunk, sets up the tripod and has barely pressed 'record' when she's politely accosted by an inconspicuous man in civilian clothing who just stepped out of a white Range Rover that was parked on the other side of the street. He produces a badge in a transparent plastic covering, the print far too small to decipher under the blinking neon streetlights of pink and yellow, but Mehrangiz and I do make out a color photograph of the inconspicuous gentleman in question, next to the tulip-shaped Islamic Republic logo in green.

As Mehrangiz is soon to learn, the Revolutionary Courthouse, which is just behind the said kitsch cacophony of a flower stand, was only recently firebombed by members of the Mojahedin-e Khalq, a particular blend of trigger-happy Islamic Socialists. The Mojahedin are best remembered for having entertained the nifty idea of bombing their fellow Iranians from within Iraq during the war. This way, they reasoned, they would incite their countrymen to take up arms against the regime, a project I always considered a little too hopeless, a little too vapid and suicidal to be taken at face value. Be that as it may, the Iranian government has long been insisting that the Mojahedin are but one rhizomatic branch of a vast capillary network reaching from Washington DC to London to Tel Aviv to Baghdad to Moscow and on to the enemy within, here in downtown Tehran.

As they walk us toward the courthouse, I'm terrified beyond belief, already apprehending the interrogations, the threats and the Montana Lights.

44

Friends

A warden takes me by the arm as I slip on my blindfold and step out of the cell. I'm led down several corridors and seated somewhere as a door swings shut behind me. I raise my head to peer out from underneath my blindfold and see I'm facing the wall in a concrete cell with no windows. Half an hour goes by, and I realize I'm trembling with increasing intensity, the muscles in my lower abdomen undergoing unfamiliar jarring motions.

In mythico-historical allure, Shekufeh prison comes fairly close to the football stadiums in Santiago de Chile. Nobody knows the figures, but everyone knows the anecdotes, the many graphic details of how before and after the Islamic Revolution, Shekufeh was the favored locus of systematic torture and countless executions, graphic details I myself have recounted many times over latte macchiatos back in Europe.

The door is opened and shut. Someone pulls up a chair and sits down behind me, while the many graphic details go prancing through my head in a wild and spirited little dance. Mambo or merengue, I think, grappling to maintain that jaded, urbane, ironic inner voice.

'So. *Azizam*. Listen closely now', someone slowly, emphatically croons into my left ear. 'If you tell the truth, we'll find a solution for you. If you don't, it will cost you dearly. Is that understood?'

'Yes.' A feeble, high-pitched croak. I sound like an emasculated water toad.

'So tell me something. The simple truth. Don't try to act smart. Please. Let's not waste our time here. Which is better?' He pauses. And I wait, tracing the spasms in my abdomen. 'Europe or Iran?'

I hesitate, but only briefly. 'Actually', I manage, 'until yesterday, I would have said I preferred Iran.' The interrogator chuckles to himself, and I can hear an office chair creak as he leans back in his seat.

'So why were you filming the Revolutionary Courthouse?'

'I wasn't filming the Revolutionary Courthouse.'

'I see. You were not filming the Revolutionary Courthouse. You were filming –' he waits for me to finish his sentence.

'We were filming the flower stand. The one that said TEHRAN FLOWER in orange. Neon orange.'

'You were filming the flower stand. And indeed, why not? It's a real nice flower stand, no?'

When Shekufeh is pointed out to curious visitors, all they see are light brown, arid hills at the foot of the Alborz mountains, with one slope separated from its surroundings by a wire fence. From certain rooftops, you can see a handful of buildings that make up the carceral complex, but a large part of the prison actually blends neatly into nature, being built underground, beneath the hills. It is hard to think of another landmark that is as elegantly 'less-is-more' and as imposing at the same time. If fencing on an empty hillside is the architectural understatement *par excellence*, by merging with Tehran's stately mountainous surroundings, Shekufeh gains an aura of inevitability. It comes with the city.

Later, in my isolation cell, it is to cross my mind that with a brief jail term and some screaming teledrama in the first person singular, both the Promessa and I could easily capitalize on the merchandizing of tortured dissidents. In most places the world over, Che Guevara as a T-Shirt, the very lamentation of Che-Guevara-as-a-T-Shirt, has become commonplace, and stirring acts of bravado do little more than repeatedly confirm the marvelous potential of the market to accommodate and acclimatize absolutely anything, particularly stirring acts of bravado. I remember an ex-girlfriend who was hired by the *Herald Tribune* after publishing an article handsomely entitled 'I Begged the Warden Not to Kill Me' and leaving the country in a media frenzy, claiming she was about to be arrested and tortured, all over again, any minute now. Unless I'm sorely mistaken, she has recently started writing her memoirs for Penguin.

Perhaps a piece on the 'Allegorical Allure' of Shekufeh. 'Gloomy, oppressive, outwardly unchanging and embroiled in a desperate and so typically Persian attempt to look intimidating and civilized at the same time' may well make it into *Wallpaper* ('Ironies of Iran') or even *National Geographic* ('Paradox of Persia').

'What is your opinion of Imam Khomeini?'
'I'd say every human being has weak points and strong points.'

'How interesting. Do tell us his weak points.'

'He had none.'

'I see. So tell me, you disapprove of the theocratic state, don't you?'

'Why should I disapprove?'

'You grew up abroad, and you don't disapprove?'

'There was a referendum in 1979.'

'Indeed there was. How observant of you.'

The interrogator is wearing a turquoise suit and beige rubber slippers, sporting a four-day stubble and an impeccable blow-dried coiffe, even after sixteen hours of interrogation, resorting to the most polite and self-denigrating etiquette as he brings tea and sugar and apologizes for smoking. Yet he is perfectly happy to scream, threaten and bang his fists on the table from time to time in a show of exquisite virility. And he is but one among many. The Iranian Information Ministry, I decide, offers the most promising masculine paradigm of our time. A sphere of innocence untouched by the adulterations of media-honed sex appeal, holding many untapped authenticities, a promise of fresh returns of the referent and tantalizing new styles.

Later that night, I look on in handcuffs as they search my Zirzamin apartment, perusing and scrutinizing everything from Moleskine notebooks to snapshots of teenage beach parties, to spiteful letters from an ex-girlfriend, asking obvious questions, none of which I can answer convincingly. Particularly when it comes to photographs of Tehran's concrete vistas or tacky monarchist memorabilia. How to explain a voguish fascination with generic cities, let alone retro kitsch, to a heavily armed gentleman who is trying to discern precisely which smoke-filled room, which Intercontinental Plot and Scheme you hail from and murmuring sweet little nothings like 'Really takes an imbecile like you to dig his own grave'.

The heavily armed gentleman points to a ceramic ashtray with a hand-painted portrait of Shah Pahlavi, posing on a US warship with his wife. 'And what's with the Shah?'

'I never liked the Shah. He was the worst thing that could have happened to Iran. I'm serious. I'm not saying that to please you.'

'You have Shah salad bowls, Shah keychains, Shah wristwatches and Shah coffee cups, but you never liked the Shah. And this is because', he adds with a hint of fatigued sarcasm, 'he was the worst thing that could have happened to Iran. And you're not saying that just to please me.'

'I mean, the salad bowls, it's retro. It's retro and kitsch and, well, jokey, you see. For example, it's, if you overdo something, if you turn it into a toy, you criticize it. You make it funny. You take control over it. You know?'

'So you turn it into a toy and make it funny and take control over it. I see. Very nice.' He points to the Ho Chi Minh postcard. 'And who's this gentleman? Are you taking control over him, too?'

'My grandfather. Maternal grandfather. On my mother's side.'

At four in the morning, the agents, suspecting the CD collection of containing information for Mojahed comrades in hiding, sit around the coffee table listening to random tracks by Dr Dre and Vanessa Paradis.

After several nights in solitary confinement, I'm no longer quite as apprehensive as I was at the moment of my arrest and discover an unexpected, growing sense of relief at the back of my mind. The state of limbo that comes with incarceration has stripped me of all my deals and duties, contracts and commitments, aside from saying the right things to the right people and getting out as soon as I can. The renovations, the fruitless goose chase for gainful local artwork, the neglected fundraising are all beyond my grasp, and I have but to lean back in my spotless cell, pleasantly helpless, if slightly terrified.

The next day, I'm transferred to a collective cellblock. Listening to my new cellmates' palaver over black tea and Super Love Magnum Mega Extras, I hear countless cross-comparisons of the many different wards on offer. Shekufeh is a carceral Disneyland, one tremendous selection of hallways, rooms and cellars that can be rearranged at will, anywhere along or beneath the hillside. Silently, discreetly, as Tarofi would put it, from post to neo and back.

Conditions are made to vary drastically, according to whether you're a man, woman, cleric, relative of a cleric, political, celebrity political, relative of a celebrity political, dealer, smuggler and so forth. Although all sections are overcrowded, some cellblocks are reportedly filthy, while others are immaculate. Some offer grass, opium and alcohol, while in others even pen and paper are impossible to come by. My own block is prim and proper and offers unlimited amounts of hot tea, fresh fruit and dishes such as chicken in pomegranate and walnut sauce, but has no courtyard, and the glaring neon lights are switched on twenty-four hours a day.

Long Road to Reform Leads Right Through Shekufeh, says a headline of a reformist weekly. In the newspapers we receive every afternoon, more and more figures of the democratic opposition are openly admitting that mass incarceration is part and parcel of the reformist bargain. Prison memoirs are apparently *le dernier cri*, as if the entire intelligentsia were joined in a curious effort to demystify Iran's legendary prisons, preparing and encouraging people to drop by sometime.

My cellblock holds forty prisoners of all types, all awaiting sentencing. I meet a one-legged army general caught with six hundred pounds of opium, and a Shirazi architect who grew up abroad, whom everyone calls Billy, who was caught with his 'buddy's stash of heroin'. I eventually befriend a cigarette smuggler from Kurdestan who quietly mumbles Shirley Bassey songs. *But if you stay, I'll make you a day, like no day has been, or will be again.*

Another convict is a handsome, soft-spoken historian with a tasteless goatee who wrote unsympathetically of wartime policies, and was psychologically ministered to for over a month, the treatment involving solitary confinement, permanent blindfolds and handcuffs, twenty-four-hour video surveillance and absurd instructions or violent threats screamed at him over loudspeakers. Yet another cellmate is a conspirator in a $2 million bank scam, who is planning to sue the government for hanging him upside down naked and beating him for days on end until he was a mess of blood and broken bones.

The most high-profile among the prisoners are three young men from Ahvaz who have made a confused attempt to hijack a charter plane. 'We couldn't agree on where to go,' they explain in raucous Khuzestani accents. 'Some were saying Dubai, others were screaming Damascus, and someone was saying Germany. So we were trying to decide and then this policeman disguised in civilian clothing suddenly just took the gun away from me. That pimp. I was just totally pissed off, you know. What a pimp.'

Since their families also took part in the plot, their mothers and fathers, aunts and uncles are all in Shekufeh awaiting sentencing. One evening, over tangerines, tea and Super Mega Extras, they tell me about last year's riots in Arab Khuzestan, a result of the annoying coincidence of being the province both poorest in infrastructure and richest in oil. Rioters were burning down government buildings until the area was sealed off by military police and subsequently brought to reason. None of the other cellmates have ever heard of the incident, and I cannot bring myself to believe it really happened, but decide I might ask Stella, if I ever get the chance.

Two other convicts I'd like to get to know, but am introduced to only briefly, are ostensibly members of the Mahdavia, an armed opposition group that strives to hasten the arrival of the Hidden Imam, the Shiite pendant to the Messiah. Since the Hidden Imam is scheduled to appear during a time of unparalleled depravity, the Mahdavia have decided they must topple the very devout and righteous Islamic regime in the hope of sowing some decent corruption and decadence on this earth.

Others are suspected of being old-school Shahists. I cannot help but feel sorry for them. The Iranian monarchists, with their airy nostalgia and *nouveau riche* frumpiness, are based in Tehrangeles, the Iranian neighborhoods of Beverly Hills and Westwood, Los Angeles, from where the 'exiled Prince Reza' occasionally fluffs his feathers and beams passionate radio transmissions to his supposedly countless followers back in Iran. Not quite the German Romantics, but enjoyable nonetheless. All in all, considering the quirky imbecility of both the Mojahedin and the Mahdavia, I feel sorry not only for Westwood monarchists but for any serious revolutionary these days. Who wouldn't rather put up with the long reformist road through Shekufeh?

The days in the collective cellblock go by surprisingly quickly, mainly thanks to friendly conversation with alternating clusters of monarchists and Mojahedin, over endless rounds of cigarettes and hot tea. The Mojahedin always snip the filters off their Love Deluxe before lighting them, while the monarchists have an obvious partiality for Menthols.

The cellmates greatly enjoy speculating on each other's cases, including mine.

'Six months, and you're out of here. No worries.'

As I take in this particular piece of educated guesswork, I savor a fierce, crushing burst of self-pity rushing through me in thick, hot waves.

'Six months? Must be about right.' A second prisoner lights his Menthol with a tiny match and blows the smoke towards the ceiling. 'Six months and he's out.'

'But if they decide to pin something on him, they can do anything. You don't want to be convicted of spying. *Khoda nakoneh*.' The cigarette smuggler from Kurdistan runs one hand over his bald head in small circular movements, as if he were polishing it. 'So don't sign any confessions or whatever. Bad idea. Just wait it out. Six months and you're out.'

'You're scaring him.'

'I am not scaring him. Really I'm not.'

'And you're doing it on purpose, you pimp.'

'I'm telling you, I'm not scaring him. And please stop calling me a pimp.'

'Alas, there is precious little I can do about your being a pimp.' The monarchist looks over at me, stubs out his cigarette on an empty packet of Menthols, then stands up and leaves, idly scratching his ears as he walks away.

'So the liability here is Badbakht.' The smuggler is once again running his hand over his gleaming head. 'Being a real goody-two-shoes. A real bleeding-heart reformist. Thinks he's fucking Gorbachev.' He produces a packet of Montana Lights and starts removing the filter of his last remaining cigarette with his thumbnail.

'Yes', I nod, conveying what I hope is a persuasive impression of someone in the know. 'I thought so. I always suspected.'

He grants me a smile of candid condescension, trenchant but patient, almost affectionate, as if he were humoring a drooling infant. 'Just tell Stella Badbakht's assistant is quite forthcoming.' He lights his cigarette, blowing the smoke towards the concrete ceiling.

Though Iran boasts several revolutions in the past century alone, popular, vanguardist, secular, religious, violent and mellow, in various combinations, none of them worked themselves out all the way, at least not in the sense of people leaning back and saying, oh, that was well worth it, good stuff, let's celebrate at that new Mexican place, and I'll finally wear those cufflinks you got me for my birthday. This may be the reason for the regime's insistence on how revolutionary it continues to be. Revolutionary Leadership, Revolutionary Guard, Revolutionary Court, Revolution Square, Revolution Avenue, on and on.

Needless to say, the establishment is about as revolutionary as the proverbial Che Guevara T-shirt on Carnaby Street, as quaintly theatrical as it is thoroughly middle-class, and this, of course, is arguably the ruse. At some point, the very idea of a revolution became so laden with musty, hackneyed connotations, no reasonable Iranian adolescent would have dreamed of letting out his Oedipal fury on the state. To the extent that reformism was long considered the more critical and, as it were, revolutionary option.

What Iran needs most, I sometimes quote Stella as saying, is not the fury of yet another government overthrow, but a 'new and improved public discourse'. You don't need self-styled guerillas throwing eggs and light bulbs at abandoned police cars to have a revolution. All over the world, soft-spoken political science professors in Burberry overcoats and annoying John Lennon spectacles are now insisting that a revolution is 'any change in the rules on how rules are changed'. A long-term, meandering, fatuous affair.

As I once confided in Stella, I've always considered it a shame that reformism ran out of steam so quickly. I always enjoyed endorsing the reformist position rather forcefully, since it offered a rare opportunity to be cutting-edge while keeping all options open. But my favorite conversational case in point has always been the White Revolution, which sounds like a Soho design studio, but was actually the Shah's sixties top-down modernization program. A blend of political cosmetics, sweet intentions and ferocious authoritarianism, not exactly a revolution in the egg-throwing, soap-box orator sense of the term. And yet, one of its groundbreaking accomplishments was to launch a new tradition of furious urbanization, with cities quadrupling every other decade or so, prompting a flood of careless, quick-cash renditions of the International Style.

Zirzamin, on the other hand, was meticulously planned. If Shekufeh, for example, was an improvised, anti-monumental assemblage of bunkers, Zirzamin was a city at the end of history, masterminded by a heroic vanguard, sealing the happy, irreversible triumph of progress over traditionalism. Colossal slabs with Messianic pretensions, standing around in the middle of nowhere. People sure won't like it, you can picture the architects snickering over their dry martinis, but they'll have to get used to it.

From beneath the lower rim of my blindfold, I see agents in loose-fitting suits of turquoise, beige, maroon and scarlet come and go, all of them asking precisely the same questions, over and over. The interrogation has taken three hours thus far. Where was the film material we shot before 'fire bombing' the Courthouse, what did we think of the regime, who were we filming for, how did I meet the girl, did I have sex with her – come on pal let's hear it you can tell us you know – what did I know about her father, who were we filming for, how did I meet Mehrangiz. And Stella: how come I, of all people, knew someone like Stella.

At noon, I'm handed buttered rice with beef, tomato and lentils in a picnic bowl. Shortly after lunch, before resuming the interrogation, the agents casually pick up a conversation slightly more gentle in tone.

'You know we saw that women's rights stuff on your bookshelf. Ebadi and Kar and Lahiji and the rest of it. Are those yours or are they Mehrangiz's?' I hesitate but then claim I borrowed the books from Cyrus. 'Look. Ever been married to an Iranian? *Nakheir*, nope, you haven't.' I receive a chummy clap on the shoulder.

'Iranian men, we're all pussy-whipped. That's what we are. We're one big Pussy-Whipped Men's Club.' In the background, I can hear several agents chuckling and mumbling their approval. *Vallah beh khoda.*

This is followed by more of the same. Where was the film material, what do we think of President Khatami, what were we taking pictures for, how did I meet the Stella girl, what did I know about her family, why was I in Kuala Lumpur last year, what was I taking pictures for. After which, all of a sudden, a very different sort of discussion starts taking shape.

'Work for us. You know how to build websites? And make video films?'

'Perhaps.'

'We need you. We need people who speak foreign languages. None of our boys know how to work outside Iran.'

I'm reminded of Zsa Zsa's stories of incognito SAVAK agents sitting in the Promessa thirty years ago. 'Gorillas in a tanning salon,' as she once put it. 'To think they were trained by Mossad. What a waste of time. Of taxpayer's money.'

'And about your friend Stella, see, we know a thing or two about her. Did you know she set you up? Did you know she's using you? Plotting against you?'

'Yes. Right. She hates me. And so do Dr Dre and Vanessa Paradis. They're plotting against me too.'

'Dr Dre and Vanessa Paradis.'

'Never mind.' Two minutes pass by in silence. I can sense that one of the men is sitting only inches behind me, while another is slowly walking back and forth across the cell, when the door swings open, and someone walks in with a kettle of tea. I can make out the scent of Earl Grey, and I can hear someone pouring the liquid into small glasses.

'Look. Let's not make this any more complicated than it already is. Just go visit the opposition groups abroad. Get the names.' The interrogator's breath is tinged with buttered rice and lentils. 'Create a database. Get us some material, some names and addresses. There'll be money. Lots of it.'

Upon which, rather than attempting to look like a hero, or a Foreign Legion *guerillero*, I haggle, lie, misquote, understate and hyperbolize, offering vague promises and obscure suggestions, until I finally sign a statement.

I am willing and able to contact Iranian opposition groups abroad and inform the Information Ministry on all that I come to know during the course of my meetings with the members of said groups.

I'm now led back to my cell, another chummy clap on the shoulder as I leave, the warden gently holding my upper arm, guiding me down the corridor. 'And lay off the feminism. It'll do your head in, *vallah beh khoda*.'

Perhaps, I try to reassure myself as I spread out my blankets on the spotless cell floor, perhaps it was precisely what Stella was meaning for me to do all along. Perhaps it made sense. Stella aside, it was evident that Zsa Zsa would have done the exact same thing. Surely. Surely she would have none of the masochistic heroics that strait-laced resistance would have demanded. Zsa Zsa, who is willing to compromise on anything but the firmness of her ironies. And on her enlightened sense of self-interest. She's a shrewd, scheming mercenary, not some gullible foot soldier.

Which is why Zsa Zsa would never allow for the Promessa to be misused as a platform for any sort of high-minded cross-cultural nonsense. Which, in turn, is why I suggested the project to Stella in the first place, over that latte, or latte macchiato, back in Houston. But tonight, I'm no longer so sure about the tortuous ethical subtexts at stake, let alone what Zsa Zsa would have made of them. As I wrap my thin blanket around me, I decide it would be impossible to untangle the correct criteria of honor and credibility in this case, at least here and now, preferring to slip into a favorite fantasy of going down on Mehrangiz, somewhere out in the Schwarzwald.

Two hours later, as I'm finally falling asleep, my interrogator bursts into the cell without ordering my blindfold to be tied into place, holding a file in one hand, tense and apprehensive, chewing on his lower lip and wiping the sweat from his brow with his shirtsleeves, leaving minuscule patterns of moisture on the creased, off-white tunic. It's the first time I've seen the interrogator face to face. Red cheeks, freckles and light brown hair, framing an anxious look of doe-eyed bewilderment. Not exactly what I pictured in my mind's eye as the silky deep voice started crooning trick questions and terrifying threats from behind my back.

I watch the interrogator open his file to withdraw a small slip of paper and hold it under my nose, a blank check addressed to me in name, the recent ruminations on credibility and the family name come back to me with crushing velocity. This is when the door suddenly swings shut, and the interrogator is trapped in the cell, alone with me.

'Where's the bell?'

'What bell?' A long, uncomfortable silence follows. 'You thought we had a bell?'

'So what do you do to call the warden?'

'Take the blue slip of cardboard and hang it outside the door'.

He follows my advice, initiating another long, awkward silence. We can hear the sounds of the cells next door, the languorous mumble of men with too much time on their hands, the occasional chink of teaspoons and small glasses. 'What do you do then?'

'You wait.' He waits.

He then starts calling the warden, gradually getting louder until finally he's screaming, banging his pudgy fists against the steel door.

Both Mehrangiz and I are released the following morning, after being driven to the very Courthouse we'd been filming a week before, to be tried by a young judge who apologizes for the inconvenience and also confirms that the Mojahedin had been filming the premises the day before they attacked the Courthouse, which is what led to the 'senseless suspicion and paranoia' on the night of the arrest.

'It's all a little embarrassing, I'm sure you'll agree.'

I briefly wonder how the judge, or anyone else, (including Stella, for that matter) might be in the know about the Mojahedin's video archives, but don't bother to ask.

'I have also been talking to our consulates and embassies in Europe and Africa,' the judge tells us in a slow, paternal tone of voice. 'Just to see what they might have in their files. And you are indeed guilty of no criminal action whatsoever. Neither here nor abroad. But I would simply like to insist. In future,' he pauses, looks at us sternly, 'when in other parts of the world, do try and maintain the honor and the dignity of our Islamic Revolution. Please try and remember this.'

He bids us farewell, and as we're leaving the courtroom, he mumbles, as if in passing, that any future offers to collaborate with the authorities in any way, 'threats or blackmail, referring to any deals of any kind', should be reported back to him personally. Mehrangiz is puzzled by the judge's remark, but I don't offer to explain or comment. I slip my check into a Moleskine, making a note to hide it somewhere safe the moment I get home.

It's early March, but Tehran is still covered in snow. During the week in Shekufeh, Tarofi left nineteen messages, while Cyrus and Zsa Zsa each left three. Stella didn't call, but then again she's the type who rarely leaves messages. Some four dozen Afghani immigrants have asked the neighbors whether I'd be hiring waiters or kitchen help for the Promessa, and the interior designer dropped by twice, slipping handwritten notes under the door. I consider postponing or interrupting the renovations, or even calling them off altogether, finding it surprisingly hard to concentrate on these matters. I try to reach the interior designer at her office, but she's never available, and I cannot find her phone number. I pour myself a small vodka. There's no pomegranate juice in the fridge, so I make do with some ice cubes.

By and large, I never fail to make a point of scrupulously making my bed every morning, then invariably spend a good deal of time with my hair wax, conditioners, shaving foam, dental floss, scrubs and skin creams, eyebrow tweezers, aftershaves, deodorants and the odd disinfectant. I track the gradual depletion of creams, pastes and liquids in the respective tubes and flasks, carefully and, some would say, almost lovingly estimating the pending date of replacement by new plastic receptacles, as if they were esoteric calendars or Kabbalist treatises, marking a particular passage of time of great and mysterious consequence or referring to some similarly momentous date in the future.

As I shave my armpits, massage my temples, scrub my forehead and file my nails, I usually peer from my bathroom window into a living room on the nineteenth floor of the neighboring block. Ever since moving into my Zirzamin studio, I've never spotted any tenants in the apartment opposite, though I can make out two Louis XV couches, an armchair and a coffee table, in an otherwise empty and deserted living room.

Several days go by. My bathroom plumbing makes odd chirping sounds. No matter how long I live in this apartment, every morning, I will always stop what I'm doing and think, for a moment, that I heard the sound of birds nearby.

Over the following days I read several John le Carrés, skim over the printed pages of an Elizabeth Hardwick without really reading anything, watch four games of Iranian league basketball and record a CD compilation of seventies Tehran mambo for Zsa Zsa. After which I drive out to her farm and sit on the roof, smoking my Golden Love Deluxe cigarettes and wondering whether any of my art-scene acquaintances knew of my time in Shekufeh. And whether they'd be impressed if they did. From the rooftop, I can see a group of teenagers who spend most of their afternoons at the farm, smoking pot and kicking a soccer ball back and forth across the courtyard as Zsa Zsa watches from the veranda, her head cocked patiently to one side.

Wish you were here. It's high season, and the Casino Carrasco is filled with elegant men and women playing roulette, and drinking Medio y Medio, a dreadful mixture of sticky white wine and cheap champagne, and all are high on Prozac, Tavor or Lexotanil. *Algunos nacen con suerte, otros en Uruguay.* Munich next week. There's also Tan's I-CON (Institute for Conjecture). Remember: Promessa as a blend of critical theory and critical practice, an interdisciplinary knowledge transfer, mapping and recontextualizing the space of the other. Along these lines please. Hope you said goodbye properly to your Khuzestani friends, possum. As for Kalegondeh: Rahati's new girlfriend is apparently at the National Library reception desk. And when are you coming to visit? As I said I'm back in Munich next week, and San will be around, too, we could all go for Schweinshaxen etc. More anon, Gestella.

As I contemplate the I-CON website later that night, I'm puzzled by what seems to be an intellectual clubhouse with an interest in a surprisingly wide range of topics and questions, points and problematics, from comparative tea ceremonies to Peruvian Trip Hop, to amputee video artists, to shipworker labor unions in Cyprus. I write Dr 'Uncle Tan' Christenhuber a friendly email suggesting that the Promessa 'maps and reinscribes the spaces of alterity in a critical attempt to call into question disciplinary boundaries and Eurocentric cultural premises' and that I'd be very willing to drop by for a visit as soon as possible, and by the way long time no see, would be good to see you again after all these years and so forth.

The Information Ministry has scrutinized and photocopied my notebooks, one by one, page by page, and will probably find a translator to work on them in due time. Which, knowing Stella, was presumably the whole idea in the first place, what with all the exasperating edits and maddening rewrites on almost every single page.

A number of the older entries under 'Networking' I now have trouble fitting into any coherent storyline. Consisting largely, as they do, of disparate anecdotes, quotes and educated guesses regarding the Shah's abrupt, unanticipated rise to power, the Shah's abrupt, unanticipated fall from power, the Mojahedin as rhizome, the Mojahedin as home-grown *agents provocateurs*, Soviet psychic research and remote viewing experiments, Glasnost, White House radiation and typhus poisoning schemes, the *Kulturindustrie* in the eyes of the flamboyantly suspicious Frankfurt School, JFK, *The Matrix*, *Eyes Wide Shut*, Pynchon, De Lillo, the technically unfeasible phone call from the American Airlines Flight 77 seat telephone on September 11, Project Paperclip, *Mein Kampf*, Mount Weather antigravity research,

Nazi relocation schemes and the Heideggerian Gestell.

Trees, I remember Martin Heidegger saying in a TV documentary on RAI Uno, are no longer felled by a peasant catering to his and his family's needs. But by men, be they peasants or tree industry tycoons, who respond only to the frame, the worldwide Gestell, the anonymous superstructure manifesting itself only through its demands upon its subjects. Heidegger was perched on a log, just outside his iconic mountain cottage, walking cane in hand, his ontological grumblings translated into Italian for the Rai Uno edition, which, in precious moments when his lip movements matched the dubbing, made the philosopher look like a wary Sardinian shepherd complaining about the subsidies.

It's obvious, predictable even. Stare at any one point long enough, and a fresh semantic opacity will emerge, invariably more attractive and persuasive than the one it's replacing. In due course, a capillary circuitry of pyramid structures, of unsuspected hierarchies unfolds, and even, at times, a puppet-master, a cosmic *souffleur* overlooking a Giant Plot and Scheme. Along with intrigues, planted evidence, pawns, dupes, couriers, *agents provocateurs*, sub-medial spaces, feigned nonchalance and calculated blunders.

I open the window and lean out until I see the courtyard below, where three girls are standing in a triangle, playing badminton. I light a cigarette and watch the heavy traffic on the freeway just beyond the courtyard, which, though dense, is flowing very quickly for a weekday afternoon.

My phone line makes clicking and humming sounds, as it usually does when it's tapped by the assiduous employees of the Information Ministry. Judging from pre-revolutionary family anecdotes, the reputation of the Shah's SAVAK was such that mere rumors sufficed to turn every disco into a potential anteroom to secret torture chambers hidden behind hypothetical trapdoors, every neighbor and relative into a possible spy. Subversive literature, such as existentialist novels, was read in daylight, behind double-locked doors, while nighttime reading required thick blankets to be draped over both reader and reading lamp.

Things loosened up during the course of the eighties, while the nineties introduced Farsi translations of Marx, Nietzsche, Foucault and Rushdie to every academic bookstore. Today you can no longer sit in a taxi without someone comparing the *classe politique* to all sorts of zoological species and organic materials.

During the prelude to my fourth interrogation, back in Shekufeh, Zip discs, VHS, mini DV tapes, minidiscs, audio tapes, CDs, handwritten notes, newspaper articles and photographs from my apartment were piled in a single heap in the middle of the room. A man in a tea-stained shirt and plastic flip-flops saying 'Xanadu' in neon orange and green walked up to the pile, picked up an article from the *Neue Zürcher Zeitung*, loudly and annoyedly assumed it was Swedish, then grabbed a Zip disc and held it up to the light. Unsatisfied, he pondered a minidisc for a little while, placing it thoughtfully onto a standard CD, to confirm the wondrous difference in size.

I'm reminded of a news correspondent, a seven-foot Polish sociologist working for *Newsweek*, by the name of San, who, one winter evening, heard mumbling, crackling noises emanating from the ventilation shaft, immediately after calling her relatives in Danzig. Somewhere in her apartment building, somebody was playing a recording of that telephone conversation and translating it aloud into Farsi. She stood in front of the shaft, screaming vulgar insults in Polish, Russian, German and English, mostly referring to prostitutes, family relatives and faeces, until it eventually fell silent.

But then again, of course, since the men in power have widely been held responsible for more disappearances than, say, Mullah Omar, Pinochet and Putin put together, some say the nonchalance is not to be taken at face value.

Brief jail terms on erratic charges seem to be a custom running through the family. Zsa Zsa herself was on trial before a military tribunal of the French Foreign Legion, for slipping an uncocked hand grenade into a sleeping night guard's vest pocket, as a lesson for the other troops. She was later acquitted.

Before returning to civilian life in Tehran, indeed just before opening the Promessa, as final architectural touches were being made to the venue, much as they are being rendered right now, Zsa Zsa worked as a military advisor to the government. This was the time she gained access to an army tank and used it to destroy the entrance gates of the Armenian Social Club, two hours after the cocktail waiter referred to her boyfriend as a 'dirty Muslim-fucker'. This, too, although leading to legal complications, resulted in little more than a fine.

Zsa Zsa did finally run into a spot of trouble shortly thereafter, following a clumsy attempt to take revenge on her oppressive boss at the Defense Ministry. The man in question was the type to shave the upper half of his moustache and wear transparent ankle stockings and wristwatches with tiny clockfaces saying New York, London, Paris and Sydney. He also installed a hidden back room in his office, perfectly concealed behind mahogany wall paneling, specifically for having sex with his alternating secretaries, most of whom were over six feet tall and had a speech impediment of some kind. Zsa Zsa discovered the room by pure coincidence, while working late on a Wednesday evening. She walked into the boss's office unannounced, caught a glimpse of a missionary position through a half-opened doorway in the paneling and silently backed out unnoticed.

Zsa Zsa was soon to realize that her superiors were collaborating with army officers and Soviet bureaucrats to embezzle government money through fictitious arms deals, and bragged to her drinking buddies that she'd give away that dirty pimp scumbag bastard to the military police. Following this fit of pointless, drunken bravado, the dirty pimp scumbag bastard used his military contacts to have Zsa Zsa arrested by Column 2, a Mossad-trained, anti-espionage unit. Upon which she underwent a long interrogation in a mangled armchair, which, as the officer informed her, was replaced weekly, due to the 'shredded upholstery and the urine stains and all the rest of it'.

To prove her case, and to locate the necessary documents to back it up, Zsa Zsa directed the Column 2 agents to the concealed office parlor, where she rightly assumed all the relevant files and photocopies to be. Over the next few days, the outlines of the cinematic storyline were carefully leaked to the press. Key accomplices among the military cadre, not knowing who'd betrayed them, panicked and started disclosing ever more names and details, for the sake of revenge but also in a vague hope of saving their own necks. The plot culminated in several high-profile arrests and a number of suicides, technical and otherwise.

Zsa Zsa wasn't freed from the Column 2 premises, however,

until an official decision was reached on whether she was to be done away with, or released under protective surveillance. Eventually, a handwritten letter from His Majesty Shah Reza 'St Moritz – *j'adore*' Pahlavi was flown in from the Winter Residence, politically embarrassing as it might have been, graciously sparing Zsa Zsa's life.

Finally, by way of a *finale furioso*, Zsa Zsa was arrested one last time, under the Islamic Republic only ten years later. Her phone line had been tapped for eight months running, as a result of which she came under charges of forgery, gambling, illicit foreign currency exchange deals, purchase and distribution of alcohol, purchase and distribution of marijuana, purchase and distribution of opium, purchase and distribution of illegal audio cassettes, purchase and distribution of pornographic Video CDs, and intent to commit adultery.

Her eighteen-year prison sentence was waived, however, thanks to a small politico-financial network of mutual esteem stretching across the municipality of Tehran, and the sentence was reduced to ninety lashes. These too were omitted by the officer in charge when Zsa Zsa discovered they shared a passion for horses, and she invited him over for a long weekend on the farm. Bring your family, it'll be smashing, we'll have lots of fun. Don't forget the sunblock, you'll need some sunblock for the kids.

The next morning, I wake up earlier than usual, switch on the Sony portable to BBC World Service, then walk down to the corner store to buy a new flask of Gillette *Peau Sensible* shaving gel and a box of Sea Pearl cotton swabs. The razor blades and the L'Oréal face scrub can, unless I'm very mistaken, wait until

Wednesday. As I head back home after talking soccer with the shopkeepers, I remember I'll soon be running out of band-aid, but decide to take care of that on Wednesday as well.

After noting 'band-aid' in the current notebook, in order to break the torpor of basketball championship reruns and John Le Carré, I take a cab to the National Library, where, in the newly renovated East Wing, I might catch a glimpse of a rare manuscript once belonging to eleventh-century explorer and poet-historian Jabir Fat'ollah Kalegondeh. It so happens that Cyrus Rahati's new lover, a nineteen-year-old art student named Mina, works part-time at the information desk of the library, and surely she could show me the manuscript if it were still barred from public view.

Jabir Fat'ollah Kalegondeh, a man most revered for his witty, homoerotic inversions and Sufi parables, is one name I wish I could include more regularly in these notebooks. *Beauty of such poise and power / even a humble Hebrew scribe / sighs for the blooming desert boy*. And suchlike.

Kalegondeh's prose, on the other hand, was far less celebrated than his poetry, and was largely written in exile, under the suspicious patronage of Shah Zahremar the Grand. *A narrator may play a game of plunging, content to know not, and yet, bequeath a word with a speaker, however weak or strong, and you bless it with vigor*. The quote, though all but completely incomprehensible, offers a self-indulgent fatalism of the kind I find impossible to resist.

The Kalegondeh citations in my older notebooks, from my days as a student in Arabic and Hebrew, are mainly under 'Travel'. Travel conjures the very core of every deserving tale in history, the solitary, wayfaring man, seeking his proper sense of truth and ethics. Future 'Travel' entries will hopefully include case studies, quotes and excerpts from travel novellas written in medieval Venice and Liguria, the Homeric epics, Crusader biographies, G.W.F. Hegel's university lectures, Reinhold Messner slide shows, George Lucas, Gaugin, Le Corbusier, *Tomb Raider*, Mirza Saleh Shirazi, *Wallpaper* magazine, Hades mythology, Bounty advertising, Beatniks in Tangiers, the Arthurian quest for the Grail, Coppola, Stella, Mehrangiz, the Old Testament, Bouvier, Chatwin, Lord Byron, *Black Hawk Down*, *Hiroshima mon amour*, Anand Ram Mukhlis, Nek Rai, Christian Kracht, recent memories of Hamburg and Beirut, childhood anecdotes and Ferdousi's *Shahnahmeh*. *Saiawush rode on undaunted, and his white robes and ebon steed shone forth between the flames, and their anger was reflected upon his helmet of gold.*

I'm greeted at the information desk of the National Library by a fake blonde with ruthlessly plucked eyebrows who looks vaguely familiar, and it takes me a moment to realize I'm looking at the very same woman with the discreet nose-job and the biodegradable Tampax Slender Regular whom I'd seen at the corner store several weeks ago. Mina seems very different now, tacky, blow-dried strands of dark blonde stretching out in all directions from under her headscarf, and looking disappointingly slender without her veil.

She is, however, delightfully plucky and flirtatious once I introduce myself, and we do not move from the entry hall for well over an hour. Kalegondeh, Khayyam, Fitzgerald, *Dialogue Among Civilizations*, the Peacock Throne, Indian restaurants.

Mina tells me about the photographs she's been working on,

which, incidentally, were greatly inspired by our common friend Mehrangiz's recent work. The photographs are entitled 'Exile of Homeland', a black-and-white series of pigeons with Sufi love poems dabbled onto their wings. To change the subject, I ask her which enticing perfume is it that she's wearing, and it turns out to be Chloë by Karl Lagerfeld, which is when Mina demands we exchange phone numbers, and I am thoroughly flustered to see her slip my calling card into her bra. I am even more elated when she impishly whispers in my ear that she might just steal me a gift from the library collection.

When we're at long last making our way to the East Wing, Mina hands me, in passing, a booklet bound in dark brown leather, *Kindermärchen* written across the cover in Gothic font, a collection of Gebrüder Grimm folk tales apparently, with colorful drawings of blue-eyed toddlers exploring dark forests in menacing shades of purple and black. The book, she whispers, was a personal gift from Adolf Hitler to Reza Shah, who, of course, was tremendously flattered by the Austrian's ebullient aryophilia, and grateful for an enemy of his enemies to be his friend. You like it, don't you? No one would notice. Come on, be serious. It's like a love token.

But when I call her a week later, inviting her out to the new Tandoori restaurant in Elahieh, she says she has very little time, and perhaps I could call back in a week, which I do, only to hear her say precisely the same thing once again, although, she adds, if ever I wanted to see the 'Exile of Homeland' series, I was very welcome to drop by at her Zirzamin studio. After the fourth subsequent invitation, all received with the same coquettish and yet emphatically evasive tone, I decide to look up another

Kalegondeh manuscript, but the library is closed, due to a public holiday.

Skimming the local online dailies late one morning, the birdlike chirps of the plumbing in the background, I'm struck by the headline of a conservative paper, 'Last Israel-Critical Voice of Europe Extinguished', next to a picture of German MP Jürgen Möllemann. I take my time reading the article, and put down the names of several sources all claiming the German party leader, an amateur skydiver whose parachute failed to open, had been murdered by a 'transcontinental scheme' shortly after sharply criticizing Israel in a pamphlet. I decide to read the online papers more regularly, seeing as they obviously hold outstanding material for the notebooks.

Another front-page article announces the pending visit of Fidel Castro to Tehran. Skimming the rest of the pages, I'm surprised to learn that the three Khuzestanis in Shekufeh have been sentenced to death by hanging. I stare at their blurry photographs on the webpage, feeling slightly dazed, and for a brief moment I feel I may throw up on the computer keyboard. But the moment passes, and I quickly calm down as I realize it's my own sense of shock and despair that moves me more than anything else. I continue reading the article to find that the hijack story was soon to be converted into a feature film titled *On Wings of Desperation*, with Cyrus Rahati playing a young co-pilot with a broken heart and nothing to lose.

Before leaving for the Promessa, I walk over to the bathroom mirror to check my Ceasar's cut and my shirt collar, briefly reassessing my tubes, boxes, flagons and flasks, making a mental note of what to replace by the following week, including the band-aids, then briefly glance out the window at the apartment opposite. As I leave the apartment, double locking the door, I routinely wonder whether I'll find it empty on my return. Remembering Stella's last mail in the elevator, I make a note to call San and book a flight to Munich the next day.

It's dark by the time I reach the gallery, and I spend the rest of the evening sitting at the edge of the circular dance floor, the oversized disco ball still suspended where it was three decades ago. Ever since Shekufeh, I haven't regained my confidence in the joint venture with Stella and can no longer discern my true motives for going through with a project of the kind. The aim, I reassure myself, is to put the Promessa to proper use. To make a lasting statement, however bewildering, and however unfair it may be in the short run.

Staring at the surfboard tables and barstools, I think back to pre-revolutionary Tehran, a place I've come to know from seventies magazines and slushy family anecdotes, and which had its own type of zest. Cocktail bars, open-air Shirley Bassey concerts, Buicks, Chevrolets, Oldsmobile station wagons, ballroom dancing, eurohippies, seventies Chanel as worn by Queen Farah – with sunray pleats and gathers, along with arabesque ornaments of silver and bronze – sidewalk cafés, fake eyelashes, fantastic political pageantry watched on small black and white TVs.

These days, you do find, say, food courts, West Coast Hip Hop, international film festivals, Nike and Puma and Swatch and Longines, along with a heavy-metal scene, pizza burgers, Jim Jarmusch retrospectives, Dutch and Korean package tours of Isfahan and Shiraz and flamboyant teenagers in daddy's BMW convertible. But you won't find a Hard Rock Café, nor $50 cocktails, nor loud Kuwaiti tourists in Motörhead T-shirts, nor Voodoo theme parties, nor sanctimonious Greenpeace demonstrations. A marvelous stroke of luck. If little else, the 1979 revolution still is, and hopefully always will be, a matter of dignity.

I begin to feel a distinct, crushing sense of wasted effort and bored futility, a *Weltschmerz* I haven't undergone in a long time, perhaps ever since reading *Catcher in the Rye* and *Siddhartha* in my early teens, paperbacks in which I'd feverishly highlight every one of the many sentimental validations of pubescent, *petit-bourgeois* romanticism with a fluorescent marker. My discovery of French existentialism, a year or two later, was to evoke a similar sense of self-indulgent, pampered exasperation.

At the time, at the age of fourteen or so, I was still living in Lagos with my parents and our nextdoor neighbor, whom everyone still affectionately called 'Uncle Tan', and his Austrian wife, a schoolteacher at the local Deutsche Schule. The couple owned a breathtakingly handsome German Shepherd named Matze who, in the sweltering humidity of West Africa, would do nothing but stretch out flat in the living room, where the air conditioning was persistently humming with Arctic efficiency. The times Matze did venture outside, his tongue a dripping quivering pink protrusion flopping from his open mouth, the neighborhood kids, who seemed to spend every single afternoon, evening and night in the street, would taunt the dog with sticks and pebbles, prompting violent tantrums in nasal Austrian accents. *Stopp set nau you cräzy*

75

boys. I always found the neighborhood adolescents threatening and coarse, and so I never truly challenged what amounted, *de facto*, to many years of house arrest in outlandish tropical environments, self-imposed.

Weekends, I would read Salinger, Hesse or Camus, or go through my parents' record collection, scrutinizing the album covers and straining to understand the lyrics, assuming there must be some deeper sense eluding me. Elton John's *Greatest Hits Volume Two* sported a particularly mystifying visual pun which would preoccupy me for hours on end, involving a pair of idiotic red sunglasses and a cricket pitch. *Burning out his fuse up here alone. And I think it's gonna be a long long time.* Hidden from view and thus long forgotten, propped up between the records, was a children's book called *Action Jackson*, featuring Jackson Pollock paintings as color-by-numbers motifs. Although I never actually colored anything in, I for some reason immensely cherished the fact that the flimsy cardboard booklet was forever to be surreptitiously, secretly stashed between the vinyl records on display.

My parents' VHS collection consisted of *The Deer Hunter*, *The Thomas Crown Affair*, *The Flintstones*, *Return of the Jedi* and a small handful of soft porn movies. I watched each tape at least once every month. One scene I still enjoy thinking back to is that of a plump woman at the movies, unbuttoning her blouse to expose large breasts mysteriously gleaming in the dark of the film theatre. She stands up and walks down the aisle to sit on some guy's lap, who takes her from behind as she faces the movie screen.

Nor have I forgotten the medals-of-honor ceremony in the

closing scene of *Return of the Jedi*, nor Robert de Niro telling Christopher Walken to 'remember the trees, remember the trees', just before Walken smiles so very sweetly and shoots a bullet through his own head. But I never cared much for *The Flintstones*, and the one thing I can remember from *The Thomas Crown Affair*, despite seeing the movie well over forty times, is the refrain to 'The Windmills of Your Mind', and my mother humming to the tune as she prepared lamb stew with red beans and fenugreek leaves, or Peri-Peri vegetable choux puffs with chilli prawn salsa, reinventing the lyrics as she went along, which always enraged me beyond measure.

One summery morning, I heard the neighbors screaming at the street kids very loudly, with more angry nasal vehemence than ever before. The kids had lured Matze to the garden gate with a chunk of meat and hurled a large brick over the six-foot wall with such precision that it landed exactly on Matze's head, smashing his skull to a sticky slush puppy purée of tongue, brain marrow and blood, tiny, postfigurative *Action Jackson* blobs and splotches spreading out across the front yard.

Travel

'Everything freezes over,' says San. 'We must reach Hamburg before midnight.' The car is crawling up the autobahn through a snowstorm at thirty kilometers per hour.

San and I had hooked up the night before, at an untamed soirée in Stella's six-bedroom Munich apartment. Stella herself had left for an Art Brut convention in New York, but did leave the keys for us at the information desk at Munich airport, with a note saying we were welcome to stay at her place. Goes without saying I even invited friends over so they can keep you guys company, very sweet of me I know I know.

As Stella's friends started showing up in drunken, drugged, squealing parties of four or five, San and I decided to leave the front door open and retreated to Stella's bedroom, where we took turns smoking freebase from a glass bong shaped into a bust of Michael Jackson holding Bubbles on one arm. We took our time going through her record collection and settled for the heated but enjoyable exclamations of a Speed Metal band from Kassel. *Fack Tschortsch Dabbel You Bush sat cräzy män wis bullshit in se bräääin.*

After finishing everything we could find in Stella's drawers, San and I started flicking through Polaroid snapshots of a seaside vacation that were scattered carelessly all over the Sterling leather club chair in the living room. Obnoxious portraits of prim, well-groomed men and women in their thirties, posing at tourist locations, from the Eiffel Tower to the Acropolis, making quite an effort to look ironic. The snapshots belonged to a drug buddy of Stella's in a silver-gilt Dior dress, who had to be carried home after tripping over someone's leg and knocking her head on the edge of the triangular glass coffee table, spreading patches of blood in that amusing, Jackson Pollock pattern over the white bearskin on the floor.

One of the snapshots, taken at what appeared to be a corporate reception at the Hauser & Wirth in St Petersburg, included a familiar, stocky figure in a loose-fitting suit. After scrutinizing the picture under the table lamp, I believed I recognized the man to be Tarofi, although I couldn't be entirely sure, since a champagne glass was partially obscuring his face.

San eventually suggested I join her for a weekend in Hamburg. Since Stella visibly had no intention of returning to Munich any time soon, I agreed, and now San, the seven-foot tall Tehran *Newsweek* correspondent, a woman with conspicuous grey-green eyes, intimidating cheekbones and a deep, booming voice, is leading me through screaming snowstorms, up sleeted highways on a northward passage to Hamburg, in a dark-blue Audi A3 rental.

Yesterday, thousands were forced to spend the night on Germany's snowy motorways, as policemen shuffled up and down, knocking on windows and offering hot tea and checked blankets.

On the back seat of the Audi A3 Sportback is a silent, vaguely Turkmen or Uzbek couple, who San discovered hitchhiking at a BP petrol station, bundled in countless layers of winter wear. The prospect of spending a night on the autobahn with San, her Chris de Burgh CDs and an imposing, motionless monument of lamb's wool and padded polyester makes me feel deeply, resolutely sorry for myself.

'Save time,' San says in an oddly robotic tone, speaking in baby English in the hope of the passengers in the back seat understanding her. 'At next restaurant: *no* eating, just drinking.' She turns to me. 'I think they're from Turkmenistan or Uzbekistan or something.'

I sigh very quietly to myself, then turn around to speak to the couple. 'Turkmenistan?' I ask, 'Uzbekistan? Pakistan?' I can see them grinning from under their anorak hoods. '*Ma hamzaban hastim*,' they chirp in Farsi, with the endearing, pathetic twitter of an Afghani accent. 'We are from the honorable nation of Afghanistan!' They nod and smile at me in a hopeful and strained sort of way. I don't answer, but slowly turn back to San.

'Afghanis,' I tell her.

'*No* eating. *Just* drinking,' she says, presumably oblivious to what I just told her, thumping her palms against the steering wheel for emphasis. As we approach a sign announcing the next *Autobahnraststätte*, Nürnberg-Feucht West, she asks, 'Did you know: I am Protestant. Polish Protestant.' She underlines what is ostensibly a sensational contradiction in terms by pointing a finger to the left-hand side of the windscreen. 'Polish.' And then to the right. 'Protestant! Me: San: Polish *and* Protestant. Have you heard of Adam Malysz, ski-jumper? He's a Polish Protestant. And Prime Minister Buzek, him too.'

Outside, there's little sign of the weather clearing up in time. The snowstorm appears to be worsening by the hour, and as we crawl towards the restaurant, San tells her passengers about the Swedish–Protestant invasions of Poland during the seventeenth century. This was when the Polish flirtation with Protestantism came to an abrupt end, and the nation reunited under the banner of Catholicism.

Waaaa-oo, says Chris de Burgh. *Don't pay the ferryman, waaoo-oh.*

The murky Nordic display around us puts me in a wistful mood, raising Byronic childhood memories. *Action Jackson*, Matze, Uncle Tan, who was born and raised in Hamburg, incidentally. Tan Christenhuber with his astonishingly thick, white hair, his St Pauli T-shirts, his comical asides in Plattdeutsch, his pickled eels and delightful digressions into dinner table anthropology. During a champagne breakfast when I was only ten, Tan prompted a nervous row with the Norwegian deputy ambassador by claiming Michigan and Minnesota suffered from a long tradition of Norwegian males running amok during the first two weeks of January.

Due to an obscure influence of bio-social genetics, mechanisms of evolutionary psychology still largely unknown to science, it was, Tan insisted, specifically Norwegian men who spent too much time alone in their log cabins who were known to embark unexpectedly on murderous rampages in their immediate surroundings. In Minnesota, over the two or three coldest weeks of the year, the radio regularly issued warnings, urging single Norwegians to seek the company of others. The Swedes, on the other hand, had no such inclinations. Nor did Danes, Finns or Icelanders. Today, you might wonder whether Norwegians would make better undercover sleepers than other Scandinavian natives, or whether, on the contrary, it made them more impulsive and thus less workable.

Upon reaching Nürnberg-Feucht, we sit down at three different tables for tea and coffee, then regroup by the Audi fifteen minutes later. After another hour of driving through wet highway sludge in complete silence, the Afghani sitting behind me leans forward and squeezes his head between the window pane and the headrest and starts reproaching the 'racism and bigotry and religious intolerance of today's Europe'. I do my utmost to ignore him, grimacing at his warm, spicy breath in my right ear. After a few minutes, the man withdraws his head and searches a bright red anorak until he finds a Granny Smith, which he peels with a tiny Swiss Army knife. His wife watches him, visibly amused.

'You're being unfair, you know. Remember the Swedes? Veeery different. Veeery progressive. That's also what Uncle Golmohamad told us last time. Veeery progressive. What was that gentleman's name? Per Albin Hansson.' She looks out the window at the misty panorama surrounding us on all sides. 'Grave and tragic would it be', she says, 'should the enemies of progress be successful in dividing those who belong together naturally, who together must solve the challenge of changing class society into a democratic *folkhem*, and who together must – '

'So *anyway*. Tell me, you guys.' San is visibly tired of the melodic mewling of whiny Asian sing-song. She glances up at the rear-view mirror. 'Where you from? You from Pakistan? Uzbekistan?'

When no one answers San's question she, for some reason, elaborates on General Musharraf and on the merit that is always due for tidying up a messy situation. 'When Pakistan government bad, when government do nothing, someone must say: "OK. Enough! *Basta*! I am boss. Big boss." No? You don't think so?' The light outside has grown dim. San looks eerie in the half-light.

It's early evening, and San announces a second recess at the next restaurant. 'Here, *not* drinking.' She thumps one palm against the steering wheel. '*Eating*. But drinking, no? Or washing hands. Meet in twenty minutes *max*.'

At this, I turn around and smile at my fellow passengers, saying San needed a good, long rest, and that we'd be meeting in front of the car in no less than an hour. At the highway bistro, I order a Schweinsbratwurst with thick, brown onion sauce and French fries. When I meet San in the parking lot, I'm five minutes late.

'Where are the other two?'

'I saw them thumbing a lift at the exit,' I tell her. 'Someone gave them a ride.'

'Good for them.'

An hour later San has run out of CDs and is flicking through the radio channels on the rental car stereo. To my disgust, she chances upon an old Red Hot Chili Peppers track. *Pomm Pomm. With history books all full of shit, I become the anarchist. Pomm Pomm. Siggadigong. Pomm Pomm.*

Although we're still held up by the occasional snow-struck

traffic jam, I'm relieved to see we're making good time and will probably be reaching Hamburg before midnight. I'm doing my best to look forward to Hamburg after all. Most of the family eventually settled down here. Back when they first moved to Germany, they used to ship their own Basmati rice from Iran. This was during the eighties, when northern Europe had yet to discover the likes of even Mozzarella and Balsamico, and you couldn't find much by way of rice besides Uncle Ben's in neon-orange cardboard boxes. Hence the two tons' worth of Basmati every February, with the stock used up precisely within a year. Two tons of butter-crusted rice cakes with saffron and sour berries.

Hamburg Iranians are different to, say, Tokyo Iranians, who are cheap labor, the Great Unwashed, living under park benches. Then there are the Stockholm Iranians, who are mostly Maoists, Neo-Leninists, Trotskyists, Post-Stalinists, Social Democrats, 'Third Way' Communists or Islamic Socialists in exile and who spend much of their free time holding each other responsible for the dismal downfall of the Iranian left and similar calamities. But the Hamburg Iranians are largely merchants. *Bon chic, bon gens. Et franchement très discret*. Nothing to do with LA Iranians either, pretentious Tehrangelinos, Westwood monarchists with their black BMWs and marble columns. The *Norddeutsche*, they appreciate these things. Many an Ingrid, many an Ole, convinced they're paying me a compliment, have assured me that we Persians are not like the others. Your culture is much closer to ours. *Nicht wie die Araber*.

Pomm Pomm, say the Red Hot Chili Peppers. *Siggadigong. Boo-wack*.

Besides Ingrids and Oles, I also know Bosnians in Hamburg.

They play arty, minimal, catchy rock music at the Goldener Pudels Klub and wear geeky suits and ironic moustaches. The Yugo thing. When it comes to metrosexual *nostalgie de la boue*, Balkan is better. San finally reaches over and changes the frequency to the soothing voice of an elderly woman hosting a program on Norse gods and legends, including Tån.

If I remember correctly, rumor had it that only shortly after the incident with Matze the *Action Jackson* slush puppy, Uncle Tan Christenhuber ran off with his Nigerian golf tutor, and the two settled down to lead a secluded life in a Hamburg suburb. But more recently, Tan had taken to threatening his lover with a penknife, in all sorts of public places, until she eventually wound up throwing herself under a tourist bus in Schleswig-Holstein. According to the radio, in any case, Tån is god of war or, more precisely, god of the formalities of war, of negotiations and treaties. But also god of justice, and of athletics. Apparently, wolf Fenrir bit Tån's hand off. The radio lecturer happens to find this very exciting.

I consider sharing the golf tutor suicide story with San, but I'm a little too drained and tired. But I have, in the end, succeeded in looking forward to Hamburg. Redbrick buildings, polite shopkeepers, ironic Bosnians. Hamburg, as Stella once explained, is the only German city which has long been free of the influence of feudal aristocracy, proudly flaunting a rigorously bourgeois identity, an unbending belief in free trade and the impersonal, libertarian public sphere. Hamburg is also the best place to buy pickled eel and herring and has an affordable red-light district, along with a fetching art scene, replete with moustaches.

Staring at the shuttered stores along the sidewalks, still drawing on the Byronic melancholia of the misty February afternoon, I try to pinpoint the last time I saw Stella. It must have been at the Munich workshop on 'Radio and Cellphone Remote Release Connectivity' over a year ago, Stella in her snakeskin boots and beaded dress by Hossein Balali. I've always been impressed by Stella's uncompromising lifestyle choices, which include her inclination to try every single hard drug on the German market at least twice, preferably at spontaneous dance parties in her own living room, to which she'll invite whoever happens to be in Café Schumann's at closing time.

Thinking back to the freebase last night, I'm reminded of the snapshot we discovered of Tarofi raising his glass in a toast. At first, I'd been amused to learn that Tarofi travelled to St Petersburg and frequented venues of the kind, but the longer I considered the chances of an amateur fruit farmer and repentant government hitman spending free time at a Hauser & Wirth, the more the tacky implausibility of the scenario, like a cheesy TV adaptation of *Glamorama*, began to vex and irritate. San is asking me whether I'd ever been to Slovakia. When I don't answer, she mumbles to herself in Polish, switches off the radio and turns right, towards Odmarschen.

Checking into the hotel, I ask the short and rather unironically mustachioed receptionist for directions. 'Just tell me which direction is north,' I ask him, 'Once I know where north is, I'll find my way around.'

The man takes a while to think, alternately caressing his moustache and his left eyebrow with his thumb, then points straight ahead and says, 'That's north'. I am about to thank him and leave when the receptionist slowly points to his right and says, 'And down there, that's south.'

'North, straight ahead. South to your right.'

'Yes,' he answers and offers a shy and frisky little smile. A true Virilio this man is. Temporal dissemination of spatiality, virtual densities of space-time.

In my room, heavily marked by terracotta walls and *Jugendstil* wrought-iron table lamps, I turn on the TV to an audio background of alternating British, German, French and Italian newscasters forever reiterating and summarizing the recent arrest of Al Qaida sleepers in New York, Hamburg and, for some reason, Milan. Their identities are reconstructed through mugshots, family portraits from the eighties and neighborhood anecdotes in Italian and Plattdeutsch. Always such a decent nice guy I'm just shocked I can't believe it.

Every other sleeper, as Stella loves to jovially point out, turns out to be a *fils à papa*, upper-class academic do-gooders, annoying ideologues out to change the world at large for its own good. UK diplomas, Mercedes cabriolets, Bally loafers.

Every few minutes I start thumbing through a stack of notebooks in my black Crespo bag, or walking over to the window to stare at pedestrians lumbering through the urban snowscape.

It's an early Monday afternoon, and I'm just about to hand over my key to the moustachioed, chronotopic marvel at the reception desk when I'm approached by a group of girls with Doc Martens, henna-dyed hair and kaleidoscopic cotton scarves around their necks.

'Jew know the why to the Hafenstrasse? Jew juss ge'iaa to

yeh? Juss go'iaa in from 'Eafrow, we did. Where you from?' They all have the same blue-green eyes of hypnotic proportions, rosy cheeks, weak chins and waggish London accents.

'Iran, yeh? You juss ge'iaa from Iran thass so weird yeh. Like vey'ave direct flight to Europe an' everyfing. So. Woss Iran like?'

'It's big. And cheap. I don't know. What's the Commonwealth like?'

'Well ah mean Tehran – s'not like Beiroo' or Istanboo', yeh? Ah mean, vey have to wear the ve-yu, yeh? Since Khomeini. An all vat.'

'Well, that's a shame, isn't it?' The conversation is presumably a mistake. 'You know female literacy tripled under Khomeini? Complex character, the man was.'

'Gryte. Get to study veh Qoran all day long. Brilliant. Kind a life is vat?'

I put on a suave, sarcastic smile and slowly light a Super Love Extra Mild. 'Righteous anger. Hip thing over here. Human rights, henna, tie-dyes, moral indignation. Funny how the victims are never so outraged. Nor as dramatic.' I tip the ash off my cigarette.

'How smug. At least you're not locked up as a sex-slave womb machine.'

'Well, thank God you Birkenstocked samaritans can come bomb us into civilization when the need arises.'

'Oh. Ah see.' She smiles, playing with her ponytail. 'Is vat a righteous animosity thing? What was it? Righteous anger? Moral indignation?'

I hesitate, and try to put on another smile, a little more self-ironic and engaging this time. In view of the fact that it fails to have any effect whatsoever, I slam the key on the fake marble counter and leave. 'Aaaaw. Now he's upset.' I hear them calling after me. 'Draaaamaa queeeeen.' I shuffle through watery winter sludge toward the city center, recapitulating and rewriting the conversation in my mind, conjuring one level-headed, impregnable response after another, the girls dismayed, overwhelmed and speechless. After an hour's walk and five dramaturgic variations, each rehearsed several times, sometimes muttered quietly under my breath whenever I find myself alone on the sidewalk, I reach a squalid Internet café, Türknet St Georg.

As I enter the establishment, the teenage cashier is simultaneously having a heated telephone conversation in Arabic and dealing with customers paying for Internet scratch cards, lottery tickets, Marlboro Reds, Gauloises Lights and Chokito chocolate bars. When the cashier, who is sporting a Caesar's cut exactly like my own, sees me standing by the entrance, he slips me an unmarked padded envelope without interrupting his conversation on the phone and continues adding up the cigarettes and chocolate bars on the till.

Back at the hotel, I rip open the padded envelope to find a DVD marked 'Türknet 2001', which, when played on my laptop, contains rough, uncut footage of city streets filmed by night from the back seat of a car, the camera shaking and slipping in and out of focus. Shuttered storefronts, stray cats rummaging in loose garbage, occasional neon lights and countless shop signs in Farsi. The car, I realize, is driving down Enqelab Avenue at high speed, passing the City Theatre, taking Hafez Bridge and eventually turning left, into Shariati Avenue. When it reaches the flower stand by the Revolutionary Courthouse, the car slows down, comes to a brief stop, then drives off again to circle around the entire complex twice. The sequence is followed by a list of names and addresses hovering on the screen, as if they were the credits following a movie. I nervously eject the DVD and start dialing Stella's number but hang up halfway through and try to think, concluding that a complete lack of logical rhyme or reason is hardly anything new and certainly nothing to be concerned about.

In my inbox, Tarofi is insisting there's an urgent matter to discuss regarding the Promessa, and Mehrangiz has written from New York, where she's now talking to curators showing interest in her 'Twenty' project. Mehrangiz's younger sister has consented to play one of the single mothers, while Cyrus Rahati is to play the Afghan kitchen help. Stella is still in New York.

So guess what. Visited the UN today. Can you imagine? Me, of all people, doing the culture tour of the Big Apple. Or would you call it the politics tour? Anyway. Our guide offered very clear statements on the artworks on the walls. We really learned something. 'This is an abstract painting – it has no meaning – it just has the meaning you put into it!' Other artworks were 'symbolic': 'As you can see, this little boy looks forward, into the future, this means hope!' ANYWAY. You have the Türknet DVD? Remember: the film only has the meaning you put into it! Ha ha. Tan will be in touch. You will find that he hasn't changed. Fatih and Türgüt tonight. Symbolic kisses, Stella.

At five o'clock in the morning, leaning against a fifties Fornasetti-style lacquer bar counter in a night club somewhere in the Schanzenviertel, San introduces me to Fatih and Türgüt, two graphic designers who happen to be the founders of the celebrated Ideal Standard agency in Lausanne, currently working on a comparative history of Hebrew, Cyrillic and Arabic typography. Both of them are wearing faded, dark blue jeans, Dunderdon polyester jackets, white running shoes and impeccable side partings. I have to catch a flight to Munich within a matter of hours, and would like to leave. Stella obviously never took the time to explain why exactly I was to meet the two designers, so I resolve to simply do my best to look engrossed in the conversation.

'So that's the crux of the matter. That's our conclusion. Our falsifiable hypothesis,' one of them is screaming into my ear. 'The letter bears no intrinsic relation to the sound it refers to. There's nothing that makes the sound "A" resemble the letter "A", in any way.' It isn't easy to understand him over the slaps and squeaks of Detroit House music.

'For the Kabbalists', the designer continues, 'it wasn't merely the words and the meaning, but the very letters of the holy scripture which were sacred. They contained the Breath of Life. And every letter was numbered. Every single letter had its number. And all the different textual fragments added up to more and more sums and subtotals referring and cross-referring to one another, in a great big, unbounded mélange of meaning.' At least that's what he seems to be saying, over the crushing sounds of a certain DJ MOTOROLA, as a flyer in the beer puddle on our bar counter makes clear. The club is filled with athletic men wearing conspicuous belt buckles and clever T-shirts, one size too small.

'So if the letter itself was God-given,' he leans in to make himself heard over a black male voice repeating *I do this I do this I do this for my fyu-tchaa, my fyu-tchaa*, to an electro-bossa interlude, 'if the letter itself was God-given, its reading was completely open.'

'You guys are so eighties.' I'm more than a little overwhelmed by the lettered drift of the conversation. This is worse than Tarofi, with his imperial grammatologies and porcelaine bananas. 'You must be the Spandau Ballet of design theory.'

I'm not sure they can hear me, for the designer solemnly nods and continues, unsmiling. 'Exactly. But so Kabbalists are the opposite of what is going on today. People sense that form is a construct, but they conclude that, well, in that case, it's a crutch, a prosthesis for content. And content,' he sadly shakes his head, 'content is secured and guarded by semantic dogma. Pop semantics and hermeneutic dogma.' He looks down, scrutinizing his snow-white Lacoste running shoes, still sadly shaking his head.

I do this I do this I do this for my fyu-tchaa, my fyu-tchaa, says the voice all around us. *I do this for my fyu-tchaa*. I try to remember something from the notebooks, anything that might bear relevance here. One brief erudite remark, perhaps, and then it would be easier, more appropriate to leave.

'The Armenians of the Middle Ages,' I say, the music once again slipping into electro-bossa, now far less overbearing, perfectly on cue, 'all these Armenians, they learned to write these miniature Bibles, tiny as a fingernail. There's a museum in Isfahan where you can even see a human hair with a Bible verse etched onto it. Today, you don't have the reading techniques, so you need a –'

'We know that museum,' the designer interrupts me, 'actually we've been to Iran a couple of times already. Snowboarding on the Alborz.' At the other end of the counter, a group of East Asian girls in tank-tops are looking over to the designers and smiling. The two look over and nod, but don't smile back. Feeling beleaguered and drunkenly jealous, I attempt another anecdote at random.

'Did you know that in Hebrew lettering, in classical Hebrew, but perhaps in modern Hebrew too, I don't know ... ' The designers are already looking down impatiently at each others' Lacostes. 'In classical Hebrew in any case the only verb that is perfectly regular, in all persons, and in all tenses, it's *katl*, to kill or to murder. And so, like, when I was doing classical Hebrew at Yale, there was an entire class rehearsing the verbs, and we always started off with "to murder": I murder you murder he murders, I will murder, you will murder, he will murder.' Neither of the two designers are listening to me. '"We will have murdered, you will have murdered, they will have murdered." You know?'

'And so, to come back to my point', says the designer with the snowboarding remark, 'is there any sense in pitting content against form in the first place? *C'est tirer sur les ambulances, non?* Is content ever more than sheer form with a little fashion, good faith and superstition thrown in?'

DJ MOTOROLA crudely interrupts the electro-bossa to introduce back-to-back Deep House remixes of the Euro Top Ten. *Tired of bein alone yeah yeah sick of arguin on the phone yeah yeah you tellin all your friends yeah yeah your nigga don't understand.* I watch the bartender pour a soft drink into a tall, slim glass filled with crushed ice. From the corner of my eye, I can see three of San's friends bending over a kidney-bean coffee table to snort two lines of coke each, using only a packet of Gauloises Red as a platter. After half-heartedly trying to catch the eye of the girls in tank-tops, I invent a story on complex codes embedded within the ISBNs of US King James Bible editions that have foretold a number of interesting events in time, including Chinese Prime Minister Wen Jiabao's 2005 visit to Israel. But the remark has ostensibly been made to no one in particular, since the designers have slowly started walking towards San's happy circle.

The air outside is soothing and friendly. I take a cab to the hotel, where I wake the chronotopic prodigy and check out, then take a flight back to Munich and on to Tehran. As I walk through the door of my studio apartment, my satchel under one arm, a Duty Free München bag in the other, I hear an accordion in the courtyard below, playing the tune to a well-known folk song, just slightly off-key.

I can remember the melody from my early childhood, when Zsa Zsa used to sing it to me, usually to calm me down during my recurrent, violent tantrums, when I would often beat, kick, strangle, or at times dismember any household pet within reach. Looking down, I briefly wonder why I didn't notice the musician on the way in, before tossing him some twenty-cent coins from the living-room window.

This Wednesday happens to be the night of the Chaharshanbe Soori saturnalia, the last Wednesday of the Persian solar year. I switch on the TV, to BBC World News, still summing up the arrests of the Milan and Hamburg sleepers, take a hot shower and fondly replace a depleted tube of Colgate White.

I open a fresh canister of date vodka, mix it with tomato juice and green Tabasco and watch the highway outside my block.

When I check my emails later that night, I see my long-lost Uncle Tan has indeed tried to get back in touch but surprisingly avoids any reference whatsoever to the I-CON, or to the suggestions I made last week.

> What you been doin ya old codga you? Ay? Married yet? I picture you doin the domestic girlfriend thing – and enjoying it despite yourself. Or you're at the stage where the grass over the fence looks greener and you feel suffocated, drowning, you can't breathe, your eyes and mind are straying, you've cheated on her, not yet but it will happen, has happened, she's an Italian girl who works at the local café you go to on your lunch breaks. It started innocently, a few nervous glances, a smirk but then you got the courage to chat, exchange numbers. Then you felt remorse, how could I do this you thought to yourself, often at weird moments like when wiping your arse after a dump. That didn't last long though, and now you're having a fully flung affair like any good Western red-blooded man will. You swine you, you smirk to yourself as you look in the mirror, you bastard, you are a bastard but I love you/ me. Seriously though – fill me in please. I'm off to Viet Nam on a holiday. Would be nice to hear from you, son. Yours, as always, Uncle Tan

Tarofi has also written again, insisting it really is urgent we discuss the Promessa. I can sense I would be ill-advised to ignore the advice of a man like Tarofi, and I know Stella would not approve, but cannot resist the petty pleasure of trashing Tarofi's email once again. Mehrangiz, finally, has sent out a passionate mass appeal from New York, pleading with half the Tehran Kulturindustrie to go visit the website of 'Aglutinador', a dissident Cuban art collective. You just got to go check it out. You will NOT regret it. You will n-o-t regret it.

By the time I finish skimming the site, I can hear the crackers and fireworks marking the Chaharshanbe Soori celebrations outside. Inspired by the heartrending Aglutinador manifestos and poignantly pretentious press statements, I start drinking the vodka neat, without ice.

The PROMESSA is an epistemic crossroads, a fashion boutique, a cafeteria, a think tank, a populist funfair, a gallery, a tribute to the New Image Economy, a retraction into uncompromising precepts of the intellectual vanguard.

The PROMESSA's maxims are:
1. Don't Cry, Work.
2. *Ceci n'est pas un anti-fasciste.*
3. *Las instituciones son una mierda.*

The PROMESSA resorts to fabrications and compromises exclusively for the sake of material gain, political opportunity and rhetorical coherence. The PROMESSA is a refusal to accept the ongoing glocal discrimination of Tehran artists, deserved as it may be. The PROMESSA supersedes the representation of representation. The PROMESSA focuses on men, women and objects and on the situations, gestures and architectures that produce them. The PROMESSA considers censorship a red herring, the true problems being taste, provincialism and money. The PROMESSA faces up to its own context, rife with surveillance, suspicion and anxiety. It takes pride in elevating voyeurism and paranoia from a matter of State policy to a refined moment of creation inherent in any relationship between art and audience, actor and viewer.

I immediately send the text to Ideal Standard in Lausanne, inviting them to design a pamphlet, a catalogue and a poster for the opening, then pour a last drink and walk outside.

Predictably, on this New Year's fête in Zirzamin, thousands of adolescents are standing around in groups of twenty or thirty, lighting firecrackers and playing DJ Bobo, Shakira or Tehran soft rock on oversized, grandiose ghetto blasters. Towards 2 AM I start running into thick crowds of cheering men and whistling women surrounding groups of breakdancers. Every now and then, someone drives by on a 125 Suzuki, and the crowd disperses.

The men on the motorbikes are members of the *bassij* government militia, looking out for clusters of people they can report to their comrades, who show up with sticks of wood four feet long, to thrash the shit out of the dancers and their admirers. Luckily, they're easily recognizable by their sparse, fluffy beards and white shirts, buttoned up to the top, and worn over baggy trousers. I'm intrigued and eager to meet these angry young men who refuse to comply with the peaceful rules of the Petri-dish community that make Zirzamin so special, and decide to drop by for a visit. Should there be any way to befriend them or, more importantly, their leaders, the aesthetic potential would be immeasurable.

Fashion

The militia's Zirzamin headquarters are in a conventional one-storey house, a discreet bungalow in the symmetric center of an open space left over between two particularly large clusters of slabs of South Korean make. In the center of Zirzamin, yet clearly set off from the rest in an unmistakable stylistic counterstatement. As I approach the front door, I make my way through ever larger swarms of young men with fluffy teenage beards and bad skin. Once I ask to see the officer in charge, I'm led down a long, unlit hallway bearing the distinct smell of unwashed socks, *bassijis* floating in and out of the many rooms on either side, and finally offered a seat next to a chubby gentleman in civil clothing, negotiating the price of a Nissan pickup.

With its fluorescent lighting and standard A4 pictures of Ayatollahs Khomeini and Khamenei, the room is very much like any government office in the country. Not too many baroque swirls or rococo ruffles, only the golden clock on the wall shaped like an owlet flapping its wings. When the Nissan dealer finally leaves, the officer pours *chaii*, and we gradually pick up a conversation on Zirzamin's badminton courts and weightlifting studios. He's surprisingly friendly, and perhaps I could even learn to relax in his presence, if I only took the time.

'I wouldn't let my daughter grow up in a house over two stories high,' quips the officer. I expect him to bewail the anonymity of Zirzamin, the size, the graffiti, the adjoining rooftops allowing you to move unnoticed from block to block, the teenage cliques, unmarried couples and single mothers, but personal liberties are not the issue here.

'Obviously it would be better, so to speak, if people didn't want the freedoms they want. But the real problem with high-rises, so to speak, is that Islam explicitly disapproves of architecture that offers a view into your neighbor's private home.' He sighs, shaking his head. 'The fabric and the structure, it's all very confusing. If you take a look at the underground parking lots, you'll see how tricky it all is. Like something straight out of a movie. So to speak.'

The man is clearly upset. At a lack of things to say, I open my bag and hand the officer a Panasonic DV camera. He looks up, a tired, suspicious look in his eyes.

'The idea, if it is not too much trouble for you, is to film your everyday professional life. To make your own movie.'

'Film my life?'

'Just point the camera at whatever seems important to you, whatever you think the world has to know about Iran. It's a documentary project. A project on the militia. Letting you have your say. After all the rumors and the slander, all that propaganda against you and what you stand for. I am opening an art gallery, I can show your work there. That's why I wanted to meet you. You just film. This is your voice. You pick up the camera whenever you have a spare moment, or give it to one of your men, one of your members.' I hold my breath, waiting for a reaction. 'This is your voice,' I insist.

'And film what?'

'Anything. Absolutely anything. You see, as all of us very well know, there's a disjunction between the globalization of knowledge and the knowledge of globalization. And that's what this is all about. Redressing the balance. So to speak.'

'Indeed. Tell me. Is this a three-chip camera?'

'No.'

'That's OK. No worries. It's a nice gadget.' After a few minutes of embarrassing silence, I politely thank the officer for his time and leave him holding the camera absent-mindedly in one hand, staring thoughtfully at his owlet.

On my way out of the headquarters, I manage to pick up a conversation with three elderly women who are members of the militia, a troika of Darth Vaders cloaked in silky black veils, silently walking the headquarters in the dim fluorescent light. As it happens, all three are simply thrilled about Zirzamin, raving on about how easy it is to make friends and applauding the soundproof windows. One of the women moved to Elahieh in north Tehran when her husband got a promotion, but then 'When we saw what it was like, everyone for themselves, nobody saying hello in the streets anymore, well then we moved right back here to Zirzamin, I swear to God, we all missed it so much it broke my heart.'

In the cab home across the Zirzamin estate, I remember a pamphlet from the thirties, printed by the modernist radicals

CIAM, the *Congrès International d'Architecture Moderne*, with the catchy title CAN OUR CITIES SURVIVE? I picture them in their tweed jackets and immaculate side partings, sipping hot tea with the *bassijis*, patiently explaining the pending liberation of humanity from the chaotic, labyrinthine weight of history, via the pure rhythms of the sublime habitation machine and its promise of a new age for mankind.

The sun is slowly setting over the enormous outline of blocks 16 to 26. The cab driver shifts into second gear, rolls up his window and smiles, for no apparent reason.

The first time I heard of Zirzamin was when San took me to the Shandiz establishment several months ago, where food is served *à la* Mashhad, a touch heavier than the usual Persian slop, with an egg yolk added to the already copious hunks of butter.

'A fucking monument,' she began by saying, stuffing a thin slab of flat bread wrapped around a slice of raw onion and full-fat yogurt into her sizeable mouth. 'Not to the genius of urban planners, no, of course not. But to The Dawn of Irony.'

Placed before us were oblong steel plates heaped with grilled lamb cutlets and two piles of buttered rice on oval platters. San interrupted her description of Zirzamin to explain the gist of Mashhad culinary customs, enumerating every calorific detail like a cooking program presenter as she grabbed a raw egg from the plastic bowl between the meat platters, slowly opening a small crack in the eggshell with a fork, just large enough for the yolk to flop down on to the tip of her rice pile.

San is the type who is rarely aware of the comic effect of explaining foreign countries to their own citizens, be it the cuisine or the architecture, the aesthetics or the politics, laying out whatever is often painfully convoluted to the local audience in irrefutably simple terms, chiding and reprimanding as if she were scrutinizing a summer salad buffet. What we have here is a decent aceito balsamico, a good choice of *chèvre*, unfortunately not enough gherkins, nor napkins. But not your fault. You don't have a history of these things, you see.

'So anyway. Why the Dawn of Irony? Because along came 1979,' she leaned forward across the table, 'Year of the revolution, yes, OK, but also the beginning of the end of orthodox Modernism. Since 1979, no ideological agenda can afford such good faith, pure and simple. Not in politics, not in architecture. Such serious revolutionary promise. I mean, this so-called Islamic Republic, it wants to be as revolutionary as the Shah. At *least* as revolutionary as the Shah. But with the economy in ruins, and the administration incompetent, and oil prices being a fraction of what they were, and the teenage generations completely, like, fuck YOU, it has to be more shrewd, more populist, they have to compromise and improvise, I mean, look at their building projects –'

San didn't finish her sentence but reached for another sheet of bread, stuffing it with a blob of yogurt, shards of raw onion, fresh peppermint, basil and cilantro. I watched a drop of yogurt dribble out the side and just miss her Jil Sander jacket sleeve, landing instead on the call button of her cellphone.

We were already drunk on the homemade vodka we'd discreetly been pouring into the water carafe, and I was considering making a pass at her under the restaurant table when San's greasy Nokia started clicking and purring at us from beside her plate. She took a brief look at the display, wiped the yogurt off the call button with her thumb and crooned '*heeeey*' into the phone, as if she were hosting 'Late Nights with Janis' on Jazz FM.

I withdrew my right leg and started blending the yolk into the rice with my fork, then grabbed my jacket and asked for the restrooms. I managed to hail a taxi on the street outside, transcribing the conversation in a notebook on the way to my hotel.

There are only six weeks left until the opening, and I spend the next five days in my Zirzamin apartment, doing very little besides talking to designers, terrarium suppliers, local papers and foreign diplomats on my phone and working my way through my parsnet. net email account, living off home deliveries of Pizza Mexiki with spicy ketchup and pasty Russian salads.

Thursday morning, I'm woken up by a phone call from a secretary of Dr Tan Christenhuber, who explains that Stella had recommended me as a speaker for a forum in Beirut, a conference on 'counter-adjusted site-specific art practices in the region'.

'Please do come over. Stella will take care of the academic side of things, and we'll do the rest, so many people you should meet, and anyway we'll make sure you enjoy yourself.' I don't quite know what to make of the invitation, but I'm tremendously flattered, if slightly apprehensive.

This morning, for the first time since my stay in Shekufeh prison, I feel like frequenting the Tehran art scene. I find myself looking forward to the fascinated, knowing looks on people's faces. Some, I imagine, will be quick to declare me *persona non grata*, nervous about the effect a 'political' might have on their careers. But even this I find tremendously flattering, in a way. I may even start this afternoon by paying a visit to Mina and taking a good look at her 'Exile of Homeland' series.

The blonde with the nose-job who opens the door of the ground-floor Zirzamin studio is wearing navel rings, toe rings, ankle bracelets, a Metallica baseball cap and a ripped tank-top with questionably obvious paint stains, in flaming red and fiery orange. She smiles and ushers me in, and I'm relieved as I recognize Mina by a slim trace of Chloë by Karl Lagerfeld.

Mina's housemate sports the fashionable dervish look – a full, thick beard, straight hair down his shoulders and a doe-eyed gaze of dreamy innocence. He looks terrifyingly dull, and at first I avoid getting into a conversation with him, but soon find him to be very pleasant, despite his sermons on the cowardice of all the young artists currently trying to emigrate to Canada and London. The dervish, I now remember, is a former student of Cyrus's, who ascribes the young man with much artistic talent and intellectual promise.

After several glasses of *chaii*, I'm horrified as the housemate threatens to play some Simon & Garfunkel on his guitar, but thankfully, he changes his mind and plays a tape instead. The housemate's artwork – pastel expressionism with occasional icons of depression and dread, a spicy combination currently dominating the native scene – is no less devastating than Mina's pigeons. Mina explains that she also does 'installations, performances, drawings, sculptures and videos as well', but I do not insist on seeing them, feeling deeply grateful when she suggests a walk across the housing estate to the Zirzamin youth club to witness a popular debating session held every Wednesday. This week's subject is 'Sexual Discrimination'.

The room is packed with nervous adolescents, over half of whom are girls. A small, perky and incredibly well-read sixteen-year-old is hosting the debate, trying to steer the discussion towards his pet theories on social performance and sexual constructivism, but only a handful of participants are willing to hear him out, let alone agree.

'Of *course* you need equal rights and stuff', they artfully concede, 'but in the *end*, there are, like, natural values, and, you know, masculine and feminine traits, and that's the way it's *got* to be.' After an hour or so I turn toward my companions to see how they're taking the acrimonious monologues erupting around them, to find their seats empty. Fighting a sneaking, demoralizing feeling of hurt pride, I make my way outside to hail a taxi.

The driver, seventeen years old at most, is friendly and talkative. As we inch our way through the rush-hour traffic tightly enclosing Zirzamin on all sides, we share a pack of Marlboro Medium and listen to a tape recording of Carlos Santana, live in Brussels. *Well she a black magic woman a black magic woman let me hear you sing it she a black magic woman* – I can't hear you – *she a black magic woman.* When we turn the corner of block 44D, I look up to the twentieth floor to see whether my living-room lights are on.

Though once again discouraged by the art thing and its idiosyncracies, I half-heartedly agree to attend one of Mina's biweekly performance pieces. This week, Mina has proceeded to wrap herself in thirty feet of aluminum foil on the sixth floor of an uptown shopping mall. A crowd quickly gathers, passersby carefully prodding her, some uptown women kicking her as hard as their Gucci boots will allow. Three young dudes in matching combat trousers and baseball caps start making jokes about group sex with Egyptian mummies, giggling hysterically at each other. As the crowd grows, a security officer starts nervously asking anyone who'll pay him any attention 'Would someone please explain to me the meaning of this work?' over and over again.

The crowd merely watches him, most of the audience assuming the guard to be part of the performance piece, as he continues to scream 'Would SOMEONE explain the MEANING of this WORK?' into the onlookers' faces. At some point he decides that it doesn't concur with the shopping mall's fire regulations. So he politely asks the kitchen foil to stand up and leave, which it does, dragging behind it long strips of glistening aluminum reflecting the pink and yellow neon of the shop windows.

I'm impressed in particular by the security guard and the kaleidoscopic exit, but only to be all the more vexed when the Golrang Gallery opening that week features lovingly pasted collages of peace signs and John and Yoko portraits. To make things even more wretched, during the Conceptual Art Festival at the Azad Art Academy, a student smears her face and arms with red paint, and slowly dances to reggae music. In front of her, a pile of bones, behind her, anti-war slogans decorating the wall. Further on, a boy with a linen bedspread pulled down over his head is seated in front of a mirror, 'WHO AM I?' scribbled on it in many different languages. His piece is called 'Sleep of One Thousand Destinies (Minus One)'.

With only four weeks left until the vernissage of the Promessa,

I still have no word from the militia. The officer hasn't left me a private phone number, and the headquarters have been abandoned for the two weeks following the Persian New Year, empty save for the devoted Darth Vader troika still typing up letters and invoices in the hushed *bassiji* bungalow. I thus have little choice but to make the SAC project the crowning piece on display, which in point of fact, was Stella's idea entirely.

After several long walks through south Tehran, she'd suggested printing stickers with the nifty phrase 'SAC – Style Art Contemporain' in gold lettering, which we could stick on anything we found attractive in visual make-up. Abandoned footbridges, police stations, grimy shop windows with glass and plastic bric-a-brac, butchers' shops in perfectly sanitized white halls with fluorescent lighting, propaganda murals, airport waiting lounges, supermarket shelves and wedding dress rental agencies. The selected SAC sites and objects could then be documented in the form of crude oil paintings, painted and signed by a transsexual, color-blind anorexic with a rare skin disease whom I briefly met in the border town of Zahedan last year.

Early the following week I call Mina once more, complimenting her on the performance in the shopping mall, and we spend over an hour on the phone, passionately agreeing on the promising, thrilling, indeed electrifying state of the local art scene. After which we decide to meet, later on that day, in the parking lot by the National Library.

It's raining when we meet, just after Mina's working hours, in front of her battered and rusty 1973 Chevrolet Camaro, and we sit in the car listening to an early Franz Ferdinand demo, sharing a packet of Super Golden Love Deluxe. It's getting dark by the time we run out of cigarettes, which is when Mina finally goes down on me, then lightly runs her palm against the tip of my penis until I come over her dashboard.

Later, as she's speeding up Enqelab Avenue towards my apartment in the heavy spring rain, I unbutton her Mango slacks and stroke her clit until she can barely drive anymore, almost slamming into a taxi which is backing into the main street from a side alley. By the time we arrive in Zirzamin, she's very ardent, kissing me in the elevator as if she were counting my molars with her tongue. Mina's enthusiasm is intensely unattractive, so much so that when we get to my bedroom, I roll over with my back to her, feigning exhaustion and staring at the wall, ignoring her attempts to talk to me until she finally gets up and leaves. Relieved, I lock the door and settle down by the kitchen window, just in time to watch her hurry towards her Chevrolet in the rain.

After opening a bottle of scotch in a spirit of celebration, I start flicking through the notes in my older notebooks. Zsa Zsa to Malraux, Promessa, New Year's 1970: *Le ton de votre voix est plein de – d'humanité. Je n'aime pas l'humanité qui est faite de la contemplation de la souffrance.* Sanskrit ghoizdo both terror and anger, Geist both spectre and mind, as in *esprit* and spirit. Entry under Geist in Gebrüder Grimm dictionary 120 pages long. *Perser ohne Hass im freien Lichte lebend* (Hegel). I mumble aloud as I read, then brusquely open the living-room window and throw out the notebook, watching it flutter and fall into the showery dark of the courtyard, wondering why I'd just done so.

This is when I remember slipping my check into one of my older notebooks the day we were released from Shekufeh. After opening and carefully shaking out every single one in the pile by the Corbusier armchair, I rush to the elevator, cursing on the way down. I spend almost an hour looking for my notebook in a midnight drizzle before returning to the apartment empty-handed.

Last days in London before flying back to the motherland Wednesday. Looks like things worked out with the producers. And I also heard that something is working out in Beirut for you, which is coooooool. Beirut is ace. So I'm enjoying the last days in Soho. Having sushi every day. Today: sushi *à l'anglaise*, which means sushi large as a roast. Difference is: a roast you can eat in bites, whereas a sushi you have to stick in your mouth in one big go. So you can imagine me standing around butt-naked in my hotel room, only wearing boxer shorts and that silly yellow Kangoe you brought along from Kuala Lumpur or wherever that was, sticking sushi double whoppers in my mouth. But trying to look as dignified as I can! Noblesse oblige. *And* there was a New Order show. I had two tickets for the suite, from where you didn't see much of the show unfortunately, but I was invited to the after-show party, Bernard and Stephen and their friends, and everyone was disguised as their favorite song, and there was this guy disguised as 'The Octopus's Garden', and it took me an hour to realize it was Edward Said. So good luck with the Promessa. And you wish me luck with Twenty. Feels special this project. Think this might be The Big One. Back in Tehran tomorrow you coming to the party in Elahieh? XXX Mehrangeeeez. PS Still shellshocked by the Shekufeh experience. You OK?

We're a group of four, on our way to the scenic Elahie quarter of north Tehran. Palatial *nouveau riche* apartments, foreign embassies, European expats with local kitchen helps and Southeast Asian nannies. In the back seat of our shared taxi, San raises her voice until it's loud enough to be noticed over the blaring tape deck. I still cannot make out what she's saying, but I sense that it's sure to spark a row with Mehrangiz, who, surely enough, takes the bait eagerly and hungrily.

In the rear-view mirror, I watch Mehrangiz roll her eyes in luscious, jeering sarcasm, bellowing something about fascist paranoia, the maturity of the Iranian multitudes, and Edward Said.

Mehrangiz is visibly in a good mood. Not only has she found all the producers she needs for the 'Twenty' project, she has also been invited to the Venice Biennial, and according to *Ordak* magazine, her latest video installation, showing blurry shots of drowning women wrapped in dark red veils with concrete weights shaped into Farsi calligraphy chained to their feet, reached record sales figures at her Paris gallery. The *NY Times* called Mehrangiz's work a 'brave, courageous, undaunted *cri de coeur* of the Islamic woman, an artist who has braved the dungeons and torture chambers of the Mullah regime', proposing she be nominated for the Rotterdam Planetary Peace Prize.

I would usually enjoy the conversation unfolding on the back seat of the car, but I'm packed into the front passenger seat with the gigantic frame of Cyrus Rahati, and the raisin vodka gimlets we've had in his studio by way of an apéritif have caused a terrific, painful throbbing in my head. San orders the driver to turn up the music, and the muggy air in the car is filled with Turkish keyboard riffs and the clanging of a cheap drum computer. Everyone except myself starts cheering and clapping to the rhythm.

We're the first to arrive at the apartment, where the interior décor is more reminiscent of Hackney than Tehran, north or south. In the kitchen, a framed banner says 'New Brutalism' in army stencils, while in strategic locations throughout the apartment, you chance upon tiny ceramic bowls with traditional motifs, filled with sour plums, pistachios, pickled eggplant, sliced celery or olives in ground pomegranate. I savor a slice of eggplant, then use the tablecloth to wipe the vinegar from my fingers and try the celery.

Cyrus huddles on the easy chair on the terrace, next to a middle-aged woman bearing a startling facial resemblance to Gerhard Schröder, and whom I have met several times before, but whose name consistently escapes me. Draped over her shoulders is a gold and purple sari, strongly reminiscent of a packet of Gold Love Deluxe Extra Milds. Rather typically for what I assume is a university-educated Tehran housewife, she has read every available Farsi translation of the writings of Khalil Gibran, Carlos Castaneda and the Dalai Lama. When Cyrus happily relates to her the conversation in the cab, she sighs and starts rearranging her sari.

'Always making fun of poor San,' she says. 'You mustn't forget how awful Tehran can be for foreigners. They're all under so much pressure. I feel sorry for them, *bi chareha*. Poor things. Must be awful.'

Cyrus flirtatiously tugs at the hem of the sari. 'Poor things,' he giggles. '*Bi chareha*.'

'And I really don't know about conspiracy theories. If you look at the British, it's fact, and not theory. Remember the Iran–Iraq war.' Schröder is smiling her Hare Rama smile. 'Cunning little fuckers, the British. With all their smokescreens and Great Games. But Americans, they just blow stuff up. Bomb everything to hell, easy as that. Simple people, but honest. I like that. I really prefer it.'

Someone has replaced the Madonna remix CD with a Manu Chao. *No es tu culpa que el mundo sea tan feo mí amor*. Cyrus sits up on the easy chair, cracks his knuckles and looks over at me. 'You weren't here during the war, were you? You were in Chad, no? Wherever it was, you really missed out. When Tehran was bombed during the war, people became hooked on their own adrenaline. Try to imagine. Every day, you'd have a radio warning, then you'd have the missile approaching the city. No idea where it would land. Then the explosion, and then the slow echo, and then the sound bouncing off the Alborz mountains in the north. That was when your muscles relaxed. So when the war was over, people were hooked. Addicted to the kick of wondering whether they were next. Suddenly all these people were buying Playstations and Gameboys, playing shoot-'em-ups.' He cracks his knuckles again.

A bomb scare reenactment, I suddenly realize, reaching for the notebook in my inside pocket, could work well as an audio installation, fetching and gutsy.

As a soldier at the front, Cyrus was responsible for warmongering murals and standard portraits of revolutionary leaders and martyrs, much like those lining the streets of Tehran. By and by, public murals of the kind, clever combinations of early Soviet constructivism, Shiite folklore and sappy Heavy Metal carnage, started losing credibility and now count as little more than decorative blasts of screaming, bloody bathos.

'Used to be art, now it's Burger King,' Cyrus says in an unpublished interview. Cyrus's latest sculptural series is a rueful perspective on the eight-year war.

I can hear Mehrangiz at the other end of the terrace, holding a joyful diatribe on Arhundati Roy, a small audience excitedly jiggling their cocktail glasses as they listen, the ice cubes in their vodka tonics making happy clinking sounds. 'Goddamn *mangos*! Going on and *on* and *on* – it's, like, *lady*, please stop piling all those *adjectives* on *top* of each other.' Mehrangiz, chubbier and stouter than ever, is dressed in black, in what she ostensibly considers to be a kind of *femme fatale* outfit, complete with thick black mascara, heavy perfume and an enormous necklace consisting of glittering silver projectiles.

'Playstations.' Still seated next to Cyrus, Schröder Rama is once again rearranging her sari. 'Imagine. Instead of doing something with their minds. You would think that hardship makes you smarter, wiser, but no. Playstations and Gameboys.' I see San standing in a corner behind Mehrangiz, an olive stacked with pomegranate paste in one hand, an unlit Winston Light in the other. Although I persistently feel embarrassed for San, I'm secretly quite fond of her and regularly quote her underhandedly, in the notebooks as much as in dinner-table conversations. When San sees me watching her, she shuffles over to take a seat on the easy chair next to Cyrus, and I catch myself wishing I had my notebook with me.

'Tehran, you guys. I'm telling you. One psycho-historical *mille-feuilles*. One fucking psycho-fucking-historical headfuck.

Cataplexy. Burma. The Fiji Islands. I mean, have you been to Zagreb? Or Tirana? Tirana is happening. But, I mean, Tehran? This guy Reza, you know Reza? He says to me: So I saw you wear Doc Martens when we went hiking. So I say: Yes, Reza, so what? I always wear Doc Martens when I'm hiking. I think he's going to say something about good footwear. But so then Reza says: But don't skinheads wear Doc Martens? Typical. See what I mean? How can we have a fucking dialogue of civilizations when this guy cannot distinguish me from a skinhead? Fucking hopeless.'

Everyone nods but is visibly trying to follow what Mehrangiz is hollering at her living-room audience in the background.

The apartment is filling up. People are dancing to a Bollywood theme tune, wagging their hips and pressing their palms together above their heads in puerile, mock Indian gesticulation, when someone finally puts Madonna back on. I watch the guests fall over each other to get to the minced chicken kebab, looking for more lime, *somaq* spice or fresh herbs, until I notice Mehrangiz standing just next to me, talking to one of the editors of *Ordak* magazine, deliberating on a downtown café that offers 'art performances' every Wednesday. Yes and so now art is mainstream all of a sudden, you know how every family used to crave those Nissan Patrol cars, now they want a daughter who goes to art school I'm telling you.

I make my way to the kitchen, nervously mixing a vodka and Coke with a twist of lime, then walk back to Mehrangiz and hand her the drink, grinning and nodding and chuckling at all the jokes, especially hers, until the critic finally waddles over to the kitchen to refill his glass.

I steer the conversation away from the subject of Mehrangiz's work, concentrating on other matters, and find myself staring at her neck and lips, then at her hands and wrists. Tehran and Shiraz, Shiraz is sweet but you wouldn't want to live there, and Tehran and Isfahan, Isfahan is fine for a weekend but you wouldn't want to live there either, Zahedan, speed or freebase, speed and freebase, Bret Easton Ellis, yeah you know how he's always mentioning these slogans on people's T-shirts, I mean how would you translate those, you can't really, that's the thing about literary translations, you know there must be a difference, like, between *Fortschritt* progress *taraqi* I mean a language is a *world* of its own, right, that's just so true you know, *angenehm* or *agréable*, modern *moderne*, *sympathique sympathisch*, and would *koskesh* qualify as an example of the remarkable accumulation of Persian terms for pimp, when I abruptly, hastily ask her whether she would like to go home with me.

Leaning with my back to the bedroom wall, listening to the traffic outside my window, I'm relieved I could make her come through oral sex alone. This doesn't happen very often. The confusing architecture of plaits, folds and flaps always leaves me perplexed and exhausted. Besides, I can never decide whether the evermore abundant quantities of fluid are erotic or repellent to me. But Mehrangiz tensing her muscles, and coming as crudely and coarsely as she just did, was one of the best things that could have happened to me, at least tonight.

Around four-thirty the next day, I'm meeting Cyrus for a water pipe at a south Tehran teahouse, a *mise-en-scène* of red bricks, ivy, lanterns, cushions, rugs, carpets, candles, fountains, folksingers and costumed waiters. Traditionalist Tehran teahouses are a popular mid-nineties thing that was quickly to rival Louis XV armchairs. Besides Tehranis of various classes and persuasions, even the devoted authors of *Lonely Planet: Iran* recommend the establishment in the most affectionate terms.

Wating for Cyrus, I try to reiterate last night's conversation with Mehrangiz, so as to put it down in the notebook under 'Fashion', or 'Hearsay', but I'm distracted by the LG color TV propped up in the far corner of the room. On the screen, a man and a woman are facing each other across a coffee table, upon which is placed a gigantic bouquet of spring flowers, with purple petals and orange pompons. The woman is a celebrated talk-show host, the man a token university professor submitting his views on the subject of the day, a recent foreign policy speech by Dick Cheney.

'It all goes back to the concept of Satanism,' he says, matter-of-factly. The hostess nods, trying to look detached and interested at the same time. She sports a gray and light blue veil and an appalling nose-job. Not only is the nose reminiscent of the King of Pop's from Neverland, it is also disproportionately, shockingly small for her head.

'At the dawn of the twenty-first century we witnessed a tremendous, tremendous boom in Satanic cults and Devil worship throughout the West. But the Bush administration, let me put it this way, when they use the term "satanic" or "evil", they don't use it in this popular, contemporary form. Their use is strictly biblical. Let me put it this way.'

Cyrus arrives, bringing an unexpected guest along, Tarofi, whom I haven't seen since slipping out of his apartment in Zirzamin. He looks frail and insecure without his mullah's robes, especially next to Cyrus with his immense frame and black leather coat.

He doesn't like water pipes, so Cyrus hands Tarofi a Gitane *sans filtre*, which he smokes self-consciously, holding it awkwardly away from himself. When I ask how they met, Cyrus stares at the TV as Tarofi goes into a long spiel on his many endeavors to support the local art scene. 'And Cyrus: he's one of the best. Very good, good nice! But listen, my dear, seriously, I've been trying to reach you by mail. I have to talk to you. Is it still welovekalegondeh@parsnet.net?' I nod, and Tarofi takes an awkward drag from his Gitane. 'Don't you read your mails?' he croaks.

'Been having trouble with the server.'

'Well it's about the Promessa.' Tarofi turns around to watch the screen. 'Bush might be a piece of shit. But at least he isn't a chummy piece of shit like Clinton was. Not that it makes a difference. No one even notices Mr Bin Laden's a Sunni. That he's saying a dead Jew is worth four dead Shiites. Did you know that?'

I shrug and order another tea. I've barely slept, and I'm also rather tired of chiding foreigners for their little misconceptions and *faux-pas*. Admittedly, the Islamic Republic encounters an impressive amount of shopworn media bacchanalia, and with life perhaps not imitating, but reacting and overreacting to art, things have become touchy and strained. But that's no excuse for succumbing to self-righteous intellectual folklore. That aside, few things are as telegenic as Islam, and the imbecility with which it's taken at face value is very understandable.

When I moved to Tehran last fall Cyrus took the time to show me around the main bazaar. Sunlight was breaking through the domed brick roof, piercing the dimness inside with silver shafts of smoky light. The air smelled of spices and heavy rolls of carpet. Among the merchants and porters crowding the busy passageway, an old, blind man began reciting a prayer. A sad, majestic, reverent melody, his lone voice cutting sharply through the clamor around him. Slowly, two other men picked up his song, answering in melodies equally morose and mournful, a scenario desperately beautiful to my baffled ears.

'Funny, isn't it?' said Cyrus.

'Funny?'

'Poor bastard can't sing. They're taking the piss.'

Cyrus is now having trouble with his water pipe. Tarofi and I watch him struggle, sucking and heaving at the mouthpiece, trying to get the charcoal going. He takes an enormous lug and screws up his face in disgust. Thick, brown speckled liquid runs out of the corners of his mouth. He bends over and spits it into his tea, which turns a milky, dark beige. 'Too much goddamn water in there,' he bellows, spraying tiny chunks of wet tobacco over the table.

On the TV screen, I recognize a new afternoon program which demonstrates the many ways in which women can make merry in their free time. Knitting, embroidery, kitchen plants. The program is called *Going Right Back Home*. Ten or twelve television screens, all tuned to retrogressive government channels, I realize, would indeed be handsome at the Promessa, lined up along the back wall, perhaps.

'The police shut down *Womanhood* this morning,' Tarofi says to no one in particular.

'Good riddance.' Cyrus looks up at the screen.

'What was wrong with it?' asks Tarofi. 'You don't support the women's movement?'

Cyrus doesn't answer.

'What was wrong with it?'

'What was wrong with it?' Cyrus impersonates Tarofi, somehow managing to sound prissy and effeminate while croaking like some demented, oversized reptile. 'What was wrong with it? What was wrong with it? You know who owns the women's magazines? All this liberal press? These pimps from the government, the government foundations. They're running the country. Used to be murder and bloodshed, now they just buy everything and anyone they need. Nice and civilized. They own the country. I read yesterday that this Badbakht guy, the reformist guy with the weird glasses, you know, he was going on about how he can get this whole mess sorted out. "Investigation this", "commission that", "committee this", "inquiry that". Fat chance.'

'What about *Women's Weekly*? Do you support *Women's Weekly*?'

The presenter of *Going Right Back Home* sports an even more callous nose-job than the talk-show hostess. She's now smilingly introducing a fourteen-year-old girl in a judo outfit, who is to recite a short poem on springtime.

I try to change the subject. 'So you think the Americans are coming over?'

'Get a thrashing if they do, I can tell you that. It's a matter of dignity.'

Cyrus has given up on his pipe. 'I don't agree. People won't support another war for the sake of dignity.'

'How would you know?' Tarofi raises his voice. 'You and your chi-chi north Tehran art scene.'

'I know. I just happen to know. They're not doing another war. And I'm not from no chi-chi north Tehran art scene.'

'Listen, *azizam*. People still do believe in the clergy. Sorry to say. In Karaj, we're building this new neighborhood library. Are you listening? When I take off my turban, roll up my sleeves, and start digging with the rest of them, we make *twice* as much progress as usual. And by the way', he pauses, 'aren't you late for an opening somewhere? No installations to take care of? Performances?' He smiles, clearly pleased with his caustic, clever self. I finish my tea, cast a sideways glance at Cyrus and Tarofi, both of whom are staring at the nose-job on the TV screen, and head for the door.

With three weeks remaining, the Promessa is now taking shape. The interior designer has promised that, with the team of Afghan laborers having grown to fifteen, they will finish the plumbing and the terrarium by next week. My furniture dealer has just returned from Beirut, from where she brought four lamps of moulded polypropylene and six clear acrylic side tables. She also pledged to find four chandeliers, three distinct series of vintage cigarette holders and ashtrays, two Ecusson chairs in original baby-blue skins and eight stretched Lucite lounge chairs, all by next week. What's more, a Dubai pet dealer has sent me a suggestion for the terrarium, drawing up a colorful blend of Tokay geckos, green iguanas, Chinese crocodile lizards, veiled chameleons, hummingbirds, lories and lorikeets and a variety of small rodents. That aside, an equally colorful mix of curators, galerists, diplomats, foreign correspondents, government clerics, art critics, magazine editors, artists, filmmakers, textile designers, furniture dealers and

Ministry of Culture bureaucrats have promised to drop by for the opening. The opening night shall be marked by readings, not one but several. Stella has agreed to read a piece on the stoning of a Zoroastrian porn star, while a celebrated novelist from Kurdistan has consented to read from his eighties torture memoirs.

The Kurdish writer was once a key member of the 'Third Way' Communists, although I'm not sure which of the many factions he belonged to. Shortly after the 1979 revolution, a 'Third Way Minority Party' split off from the rest of the group and opted for armed underground resistance against the newly-founded Islamic regime. The remaining 'Third Way Majority' faction, in turn, soon split into a 'Majority of the Third Way Majority', which was trying to actively collaborate with the regime, and an 'Alternative Minority of the Third Way', which preferred not to. The 'Majority of the Third Way Majority' was disintegrating even further, into the 'Pacifist Alternative Minority of the Third Way', the 'Democratic Alternative Majority of the Third Way Majority', the 'Democratic Majority of the Third Way Majority' and the 'Bolshevik Devotion Society', when the cadres of all the factions were hunted down, arrested and, in most cases, executed by Tarofi and his colleagues. The Kurdish novelist only escaped execution by insisting, even under physical torture, that there had been some kind of mistake and that he'd never even heard of the 'Third Way' in the first place.

To follow the novelist, I've invited an African-American Muslim from Baltimore, a soft-spoken woman with a passion for sixties road movies and good Turkish coffee. The Baltimore Muslim fled the US for Tehran in 1980, after disguising herself as a DHL delivery employee and shooting the former Iranian ambassador in the forehead. She has since spent her time in Iranian exile, regretting that Baltimore morning with increasing bitterness and desperation. By way of a title for her reading, I suggested she choose 'Return To Sender', but it appears she will stick to 'Iran: A Democracy Betrayed'. I briefly consider inviting the Isfahan University Re-enactment Society, which specializes in staging historical battles in public parks and community centers, to reconstruct the Baltimore shooting at the Promessa but decide against it. Stella would most probably disapprove. By way of a token academic, she has suggested I invite Uncle Tan Christenhuber himself.

When Stella first met Christenhuber in 1991, the two reportedly spent an entire evening sipping single malt whiskey and discussing various remote detonation technologies as allegories for the Globalization of Knowledge. Apparently, the evening ended with a midnight discussion on 'the creative Muslim psyche'. The 'creative Muslim psyche', Stella was later to quote Uncle Tan, sought seclusion and privacy, while the 'destructive Muslim psyche' needed to surround itself with witnesses of its doing, for it destroyed even the traces of its own work. The destructive psyche was comfortable among onlookers precisely because it did not mind being misunderstood. It could even accept the possibility of everything going completely wrong at any moment, for its one preoccupation was fresh air and open space, and the 'entitlement to destruction' that pervaded, organized and accommodated everything before it.

Something in the tone of Stella's voice suggested that perhaps things did not end with one last single malt and a polite peck on the cheek. So I claimed the entire spiel was stolen, *tel quel*, from a late Walter Benjamin essay, and whenever Stella mentions Christenhuber I invariably sigh and shake my head, disgusted by the intellectual frivolity of it all.

What is more pressing than a celebrity academic, I suggest to her, is some resemblance of a thematic backdrop, not for the audience or the contributors necessarily, but for the brochure, the trilingual catalogue and the international e-flux press release. Spectacles of Simulacrum and Struggle. Perhaps. Simulacral Spectacles of Struggle. If I Can't Google, I Don't Wanna be Part of Your Revolution. Beyond East/West: Remapping Aesthesis as the Dismemberment of Sheharazade. Every Time a Good Time: Resistance in the Age of Mechanical Reproduction.

Administration

It's dark when I wake up to catch the Middle East Airlines flight to Beirut, just a vague trace of blue on the horizon, but the traffic already reassuringly heavy on the highway outside my window. I switch on MTV Asia Kickstart, shower to the ambrosial sounds of chirping pipes and faucets, make myself a sweet Turkish coffee and call a cab. As I walk out of the main entrance to block 44D, I see my neighbors standing by the doorway in groups of three or four, talking in hushed voices. A teenager who flunked his high-school graduation exams just threw himself off the rooftop. Did I want to take a look? I hesitate as I consider the offer, but in view of the traffic I decide I'd better leave.

The cab driver is the same young Brezhnev in the polyester suit who drove us to Karaj only weeks ago, the Neil Diamond tape still playing in the Samsung stereo.

It's past noon in Beirut. I'm sitting in the lobby of the Hotel Continental, waiting for Uncle Tan, who is to meet me for an afternoon tea. An unobtrusive hotel, baroque, some art deco, small white cases suspended on the walls displaying Patek Philippe Calatrava 5120 and framed color photographs of national tourist attractions. The employee at the reception faintly resembles the chronotopic marvel from the hotel in Odmarschen, Hamburg, if much taller and decidedly more handsome. I've never been to Beirut before. The stereo is actually playing Feiruz. *Meyteh a'lah beera, habibi*, says Feiruz. *Meyteh a'lah beera.*

The forum is taking place at the time of yet another military onslaught on Palestinian cities, and everyone has heard the story of how Dr Tan Christenhuber, visiting an artist's studio in Ramallah, had to heroically sneak through lines of Israeli tanks to reach Beirut, braving death or imprisonment or worse.

As he walks into the lobby, I can see he's wearing a black corduroy suit and the same felt hat he had on for the TF1 interview. His hair has grown, along with his beard, and I now remember that when I first saw his picture in the festival catalogue, I mistook him for Kris Kistofferson.

'I feel so incredibly guilty,' he moans as he lets himself flop down into an armchair next to me. 'So. Incredibly. Guilty. Sitting here babbling about the history of photography and this and that and this and that. And in Jenin and Ramallah you get shot for carrying out the trash.'

I look down at the green and khaki wall-to-wall carpeting, then glance shyly over at Tan, whose familiar, droopy eyelids still make him look like he's fighting the urge to fall asleep. I nod, waiting for some sign of recognition, of family complicity. But he carries on without blinking.

'I mean, half the art scene is at the demonstrations. All of them telling me it's nonsense to be chatting about aesthetics at a time like this.' He suddenly raises his head and laughs at the ceiling, as if giggling at a private joke.

I offer a small handful of conversational schemes on the subject of art and politics, most of which I remember from my Moleskines, particularly the ones under 'History'. Tan watches me with sleepy eyelids, and just as I think he's about to recognize me, he continues, 'In Ramallah, a tank unit just destroyed the photo archives. Historical photos of everyday life before the Israelis. Historical photos that didn't correspond to the founding myth of the nation of Israel. Which goes a little something like this: "Before us, there were only idle Arabs lying around in camel dung." So Ramallah's Center for Photography was blown to bits, along with its archives.' Tan is not as angry or emotional as one might expect. He may just as well be explaining a ripped sleeve on his Burberry overcoat.

I've always been intrigued by the amount of attention Palestine has successfully generated, more than Ethiopians, Kurds, Chechens, Chiapans, Bolivian coca farmers and Tibetan monks put together. Not to mention the Iraqis. Back in the nineties, a million Iraqi minors casually starved to death by UN sanctions or blown to humus by Clinton's weekly air raids weren't enough to make it onto the mainstream circuit. But all you needed were a small handful of Palestinians, a hundred casualties a year would do fine, and you had half the students in the northern hemisphere walking around in red-and-white *kaffieh* neckscarves. Encouraged by Tan's pragmatic air of nonchalance, I'm about to ask him about this ingenious example of media promotion but decide against it.

My presentation was written entirely by Stella, and I haven't taken the time to study her paper in the plane as I'd intended. I urgently need to read the text at least once and, that aside, I would like to offer something more personal by way of an introduction, something flip and self-ironic, about the little things which lend Mid-East art scenes a gauche and untimely touch. Not unlike MTV Hip Hop tycoons proving street credibility by yelling Murder Incorporated and nigguh, I aint frontin, you one dead nigguh, from cruise ships and helicopter landing platforms. The idea was to introduce the talk with a first-hand account of a north Tehran cocktail party. A suave, light-hearted and yet vaguely moralistic, self-righteous sort of spiel, a hint of Hezbollah, a sprinkle of Evelyn Waugh.

But now I'm not so sure. On the one hand, war crimes and suicide bombings, on the other, the Tehran cocktail party. How trite. A discursive *Medio y Medio* at best. In my breast pocket I can feel the contours of the speech, which I'd meant to rehearse in front of my bathroom mirror in Zirzamin. I fondle the edges, somewhat disgusted, as if it were a cyst or a skin disease. Tan suggests a drive to some pan-Arab photo institute, and I half-heartedly agree. Outside, the passersby look relaxed and sweet-tempered despite the late-afternoon drizzle.

At the institute, we drink sweet coffee and cardamon with a video artist dressed in motorcycle goggles and a black leather outfit, and hear of the difficult search for sponsors and the impossibility of relying on the Ministry of Culture. I cannot stop thinking about my cyst. Soon, it's 5 PM, and I still haven't returned to the Continental to study Stella's talk, but we're already moving towards a bar, so let's have an apéritif, have you tried Lebanese arak, it's great, *a'n jad*, and so I tag along, but keep running my fingertips over the bump on my breast. The talk begins in seventeen hours precisely.

The bar is known to be frequented by cheerful constituents of the ageing communist intelligentsia, drinking arak and watching TV, tuned to a Hezbollah channel, just like every other television set I've seen so far. I watch them drink, realizing this is precisely what the Neo-Leninists and Stalinists, Trotskyists and Maoists in Zsa Zsa's cellar must have looked like. Copious moustaches, exhausted demeanors, V-neck sweaters.

I'm introduced to some of the art crowd, including several dark-skinned women with stern, elegantly sculpted features, almost Eritrean in character. Not like the Eritreans from the famine reports, but like the ones at food stands at music festivals in Munich or Glastonbury. By comparison, most of the men look surprisingly bland, precisely the type to stand in line in Munich or Glastonbury for overpriced Eritrean mutton sauce in a sourdough crêpe. Tan and some of the forum participants huddle in a corner by the door, drinking beer or Ballantine's.

Sharon, Ramallah, the photo archives, past massacres, coming massacres, ongoing massacres, massacres *tout court*, friends and family who have wondered aloud about the pros and cons of blowing themselves up in a supermarket in downtown Tel Aviv. Europe will never do anything about anything. We need another 9/11. Just one, then they'll get it. Perhaps.

No but the Americans should come over I swear, *a'n jad*, they should occupy everything. Two advantages. Listen. One. We get rid of all our Arab leaders. Two. Once the Americans are on the ground, we can shoot them.

I'm reminded of the images of dancing Palestinian children that went around the world immediately after 9/11. Many a liberal-minded progressive found the pictures were not representative. Propagandist, racist bigotry against the nicer Muslims, and most of them were, they insisted, clearly nice. It soon turned out the images were actually taken from older archives dating back to Desert Storm, and a senior BBC official stepped down in protest. Then again, someone back at the Elahieh cocktail party claimed the images were proven authentic after all, and that they were now suing the official who'd stepped down.

9/11 was great. We could hardly believe it. Everyone took time off and got drunk with the communists in front of the TV. One stupid crack after another. Rarely laughed so much in my life. So can I get you a different whiskey this time no I'm sticking to Ballantine's what kind of a whiskey is that well whatever it's my drink OK? I can hardly concentrate, for I'm constantly laying my right hand on my left breast pocket, as if practising the traditionally mannish-Mid-Eastern manner of greeting.

Seventeen hours later I'm standing at the front of a large, half-filled auditorium with ridiculously bright lights shining in my eyes. Sitting in the front row, I can make out a small crowd of Iranian diplomats, all in flabby, oversized dinner jackets and collarless white shirts, comfortably fondling their standard six-day stubble. Tan had warned me about the delegation, but I don't mind in the slightest. On the contrary, its presence provides a perfect touch of geopolitical bearing.

I start with a coquettish remark regarding my being the only non-Arab speaker at the forum. Then another, equally superfluous comment comparing the Promessa to an exotic pack of foreign cigarettes you place on a bar counter, and which allows you to start a conversation with people you'd otherwise never meet, only to encounter a silence emanating from beyond the floodlights. Still trying to win over the audience, I go over a choice selection of carefully intellectualized Tehran art gossip.

Mehrangiz's laughable taste in film and video, for example, which 'perfectly mirrors and matches her dress sense', the nose-jobs at the openings, the conceptual art festival and such.

'You see, the basic problem is not censorship per se, but the provincialism through which we view the international cycle of supply and demand.'

At this, the Iranian ambassador bursts into applause, demanding I repeat the statement in Farsi, so his colleagues can understand.

I then unfold Stella's text for the first time, furtively skimming the first page as I pretend to clean my glasses on the sleeve of my navy blue Fendi suit, slightly taken aback as I encounter what seems to be a catalog of pointed speculations on links between Aryan mythology and the founding of Israel.

'These historical links', the introduction sanctimoniously reads, 'will once and for all effectively dispel a staggering number of persistent misunderstandings. What else can one do in this day and age but repeatedly refer to our misguided histories of arrogance and bloodshed, in the hope of never repeating them again?'

Stella, I assume, was high on the newest rendition of Munich amphetamines when she wrote this, but I do my best to peer grimly into the floodlights and ceremoniously put on my glasses as I begin the lecture.

'When it comes to the Holy Bible, the most popular stories are the first myths: Paradise, Babel, Noah's Ark, the first nomads, Sarah and Abraham and Moses and the return to the Promised Land, before we get to Joseph's Virgin and such. What is striking, however, is that the gap between Moses and Mary amounts to a period of six centuries, during which Israel was colonized by Persia for several hundred years. And nothing, apparently, really happened during this time. On the contrary. The Persians politely invited the Jews back home from exile in Babylon, to live in peace and do their thing, exactly the way they liked it. The *Pax Iranica* as Hebraism's golden age. And since peace is boring, it's no wonder neither Ezra nor Nehemia are major characters in kindergarten coloring books.

But Persian statesmen were also known for their shrewd identity politics for imperial ends, using unflinching methods of forced resettlement to ghettoize entire populations. The ethnic units thus created could hold their proper cults and emblems, which appeased anti-Persian sentiment, and were assigned specific economic functions, which permitted a more efficient administration of the imperial body.

The Jewish returnees from Babylonian exile formed a fraction of the local population but were granted exclusive privileges by the Persian imperial authorities. Political spokesmanship, land rights, the official cult. If they didn't control the local intermarriages, the regional paganisms and oral histories, they had the archives and the land grants, along with any other written records, for that matter.

A cult of the forefathers emerged among the Jewish returnees during this era, a shift towards kinship rather than territory.

Lineage is the better way to clearly define who is clearly Jewish and to lay claim to land one possessed a long time ago.'

Stella's talk now launches into a barrage of Bible stories exemplifying the move from territorial paradigms to mythologies of kinship, then offers a comparison of the Jewish and Persian godheads of the time, portraying Moses and the Zoroastrian Ahura Mazda as uneasy bedfellows who nonetheless settled on a number of matters, like monothcism, personal answerability and rabid doctrines of racial supremacy. Cross-racial proselytism was not exactly *de rigeur* among the Persians, nor among the Jews. Much as Ahura Mazda is not a universal God, but God of the Aryans only, YHWH is the exclusive God of the children of Israel.

Several millennia later, Stella's lecture finally concludes, and prophet Zoroaster is rediscovered and popularized by the same cultured celebrities in silly wigs and fluffy shirtsleeves who devised the European understanding of the Aryan myth.

Within an hour, I'm sitting in a taxi with Uncle Tan, on the way to some restaurant. Like some over-eager, compulsive bookkeeper, I'm already looking forward to putting down Stella's Perso-Israeli ruminations in my Moleskine, adding them to my already sizeable index of opaque branches of quasi-colonial conspiracies and capillary ideological networks to be narrativized in my next notebook, under 'Gossip' presumably.

We can have an apéritif at the bar, *yalla habibi*, it'll be really nice, *a'n jad*. Tan, who has clearly developed a habit of relentlessly repeating the few Arabic turns of phrase he can muster, is obviously pleased with me. Or with Stella, rather. He keeps smiling, shaking his head and whispering sweet nothings at the car window. 'Stella, Stella' and 'Stellastellastella.' The temptation to call Uncle Tan's bluff, to demand he stop pretending he's never seen me before, or to at least get to the bottom of that revoltingly congenial email referring to my wife, my Italian lover and whatnot, is excrutiating. But it's unlikely Stella would approve of any confrontations or family reunions at this stage, so I prefer to restrain myself. Stella aside, it's impossible to tell whether Christenhuber has failed to recognize me or merely chosen not to.

When he asks me whether I had any idea of what Stella was trying to imply with the talk – 'I mean in the overall scheme of things' – I have to answer that no, I didn't, not really, and Tan turns back to the window, once again softly chuckling at the persistent evening drizzle outside.

The restaurant turns out to be an enormous, rectangular cube of brute concrete with a single, long dinner table running through the center. Hovering high above the table, in midair, is a massive steel tube. After taking the elevator, I realize that this suspended steel contraption contains the restaurant bar within.

Having ordered our drinks, seated about halfway down the tube, I question Tan on the enigma of Palestinian public relations. He takes a moment to smile and scrutinize me, then slowly goes through a small list of possibilities, ranging from seventies relations to the European intelligentsia, including the *Rote Armee Fraktion*, to latent post-Balfour guilt, to a quasi-Biblical concern for the region.

'Jesus was, after all, a Palestinian,' he mumbles into his Tanqueray and tonic. 'But *à propos* public relations. I'm not into this knee-jerk game of show and tell anyway *habibi. A'n jad.* And

I don't think understanding is possible in the first place. What we can hope for is some kind of emotional empathy. But not an awareness of the situation on the ground. Nor of the subjectivities at stake.' He peers through the tiny slits in the steel paneling at the restaurant below. 'But maybe awareness or understanding don't have anything to do with it. What can I tell you?'

Dr Tan Christenhuber smiles once again, raising his eyelids just a touch. 'In any case, why should all that bother you? It's your job, in a way. It's your job to run around the comfy corridors of power deconstructing geographic metaphors and allegories of colonialism in Gaugin and Pocahontas and all that. It's not for you to worry about everyday problems in these parts of the world.'

'Well, I'm glad some people are more into the corridors of power than running around with lovable intentions listening and understanding and comparing and taking off their shoes and sitting cross-legged in mud huts sipping pepper soup with Ali and Fatima.'

'Might actually do you some good, *hayati*.' He smiles, raising his eyebrows at me as he sips on his Tanqueray and tonic.

I stand up from the barstool and brush past Tan, causing him to drop his glass, then turn around and kick it across the corridor to the far end of the bar, small, glittering chunks of ice, glass and lemon spraying out in all directions. I instantly regret the gesture, but proceed to the elevator and make my way out.

In Lagos, our family villa by the lagoon had steel bars on all the windows and padlocked metal doors in strategic places throughout the house. My bedroom was on the second floor.

One morning, towards 3 AM, restless and tense after lying awake for five hours listening to the loud, steady burr of the air-conditioning, I stood up and walked over to the window. I peered down through the steel bars into the parking lot, where the night guard usually sat dozing on a green lawn chair or reading Frederick Forsyth novels. The night guard was an illegal immigrant from Chad.

I was amazed to see the night guard lying on his back under a thick blanket, sweating heavily, his face contorted as he frantically fondled his crotch. I watched him for a while, then hurried across the room to my desk, picked up a domino stone and took aim as well as I could through the bars across the window. When the domino hit him on the cheek, the night guard immediately pulled up his trousers, threw off the blanket, and started hurrying up and down the entire length of the compound, looking for the trespasser. Eventually he gave up and took to disbelievingly searching the cloudy night sky, still clutching the domino stone in one hand. I felt very pleased with myself as I fell asleep, and the next day I walked up to the guard, waved a domino in his face and laughed.

'Remember last night?' I asked, bouncing the wooden object up and down on the palm of my hand, 'You do remember, don't you?'

Several years later I was to visit the neighborhood once again, on a nostalgic holiday trip with my parents. As we were having an afternoon coffee with our former neighbors, enjoying their Schlaatemer Rickli pastries dusted with sugar, fresh from Basel, we were told about a recent armed robbery in the compound. Apparently, the day after that robbery, our one-time night guard, the one with the toothy smile, what was his name, the fellow from Chad, poor guy, well he had neither an alibi nor a residency permit to show for himself, so he was arrested as a scapegoat, and shot without trial, poor guy. Remember how sweet that boy was, he used to gobble those malaria tablets four at a time, primaquine, or was it chloroquine.

It's raining in Tehran, and the whole city smells of wet concrete dust, like a moist sleeping bag. Or a paperback novel that hasn't been opened in decades. I call Mehrangiz, who patiently listens to me elaborate on Lebanese seafood, the video artist in black leather, the talk, the diplomats, the eerie encouter with Uncle Tan. She then apologizes for not having much time, but perhaps I could call her again the next day. Slightly piqued by what I take to be a demonstrative show of indifference, I call her at half-past seven the next morning. Did I wake you? Hope I didn't wake you. Sorry.

When she hangs up on me, I redial her number, only to hear an infuriating busy signal. After five consecutive attempts to reach her, I take a cab to block 39A, where I run up the stairs to her eighteenth-story apartment. Seeing as she refuses to open the door, I make a deafening scene in the hallway, buzzing the doorbell, kicking the door and screaming incoherent threats and sexist insults until the neighbors ask me to leave.

'And so on and so forth, buzzing the doorbell, kicking the door and screaming until Mehrangiz's neighbors threaten to call the cops.' I'm having lunch with Tarofi at the Bol Bol Burgers branch on Vali 'Asr Square. 'The neighbors were all, like, you better get out of here, young man.' Tarofi is once again dressed in his clergyman's garb and Kojak sunglasses. We're seated by a window overlooking the square, with its grubby water fountains set in enigmatic geometric configurations, and its gaudy Dubai-inspired façades. I'm having a Ceasar salad, while Tarofi is chewing on a Pizza Special. He scoffs and jeers at me for my early-morning tantrum, what a touchy oriental soul you are, then abruptly changes the subject. 'So the reason I've been trying to reach you all this time.'

Tarofi has been talking to his friends among the upper echelons of the cultural bureaucracy, and the Promessa, they have assured him, won't last long without the appropriate official backing. I had best pay a visit to the Ministry of Culture, where I could get in touch with old acquaintances and secure all the suitable stamps, seals and signatures for the file. 'Oh and Badbakht will want the envelope with the Türknet DVD,' Tarofi croaks. 'Just leave it with his assistant.'

'Are you sure it's necessary?'

'Sure what is necessary?'

'All this paperwork.'

'Of course it's necessary. How long have I been trying to tell you this?'

'I thought that in an oral culture, contracts don't mean anything.'

'You're starting to sound like that *Newsweek* correspondent. San or Tan or whatever her name is.'

'I was joking.'

'Good.' We finish our Zam Zam colas, watching tired businessmen chew on pizzaburgers and mumble into their cellphones. Petite students in white headscarves and thick makeup sit with their boyfriends, mostly wearing light-blue imitation Ralph Laurens and slicked-back hair. I cannot think of anything to say. 'I like your new cape. The blue, it suits you.'

'Thanks. Whatever.'

Walking out of the restaurant, I'm once again mesmerized by the airy elegance of Tarofi's clerical robes wafting down the aisles, climactic Tehran soft rock in the background. None of the other customers seem to notice.

As we part outside the diner, Tarofi raises his sunglasses to look deep into my eyes. 'And don't worry about a thing. Just look into the matter tomorrow morning, and everything will be fine. And then give me a call next week, I'll be back from Rotterdam. Very good nice.'

I offer all the standard formulae of gratitude and self-denigrating humility I can think of, promising to call him next week, then take a long walk down Enqelab Boulevard, past countless shoe stores, another Bol Bol Diner, the City Theatre, and the cat-calling transvestites off Hafez Avenue and Student's Park, which is filled with cruising gay men, but also with families and straight teenage couples who do not seem to know, or care.

I buy a plastic cup of thick, unsweetened honeydew melon juice and sit on a concrete bench, watching the six-lane traffic through the oak trees along the sidewalk. Sitting at the other end of the park bench is a veiled woman in her forties, clutching a leather shoulder bag that says 'Bye Bye Kitty' in bright red. We sit silently side by side on the bench for roughly fifteen minutes, then I finish my juice and take a cab back home, reminding myself to check the lights in my apartment from afar as we approach Zirzamin.

Carrying the padded envelope with the Türknet DVD in my inside pocket, I spend the next two days visiting one government office after another, chasing Tarofi's contacts (Mr Badbakht? He has just left for Tabriz. I'm so sorry.) or bartering with their substitutes (Can't do anything for you without the consent of the honorable Mr Badbakht, but you might try Mr Kambakhsh.) and drinking black tea, shaking hands and smiling as I politely answer endless questions on European, US and African conceptions of Iran and discussing Hobbes, Hayek, Popper and Wittgenstein, whom the bureaucrats like to quote with an affected and mildly ostentatious air about them, particularly the testy, self-conscious Kambakhsh, in his notoriously oversized, thick-rimmed reading glasses. Really it would be wonderful if I could just have ten minutes of Mr Badbakht's time, or could you at least give him this envelope when you see him, thanks so much.

The bureaucrats draw fleeting comparisons between thinkers Persian and Arabic, though without discussing the latter in detail, assuming I do not know a thing about them, which indeed I do not. So they prefer to ask for entertaining comparisons between Tehran and Munich, Tehran and Togo, Tehran and LA – and so what do you prefer, Iran or the US? – and then move on to extensive questioning regarding the multifarious opposition groups in Berlin, Hamburg and Stockholm, until I've assembled all the stamps, signatures, government health warnings, public safety certificates and gallery permits I think I might possibly need.

Later that day, I receive an email from Tan Christenhuber's personal assistant at the Zurich I-CON, saying the Promessa project looks 'interesting as well as engaging'. Unfortunately, however, a colleague is already covering the Middle East, a doctoral thesis on the politics of queering in public baths in Tangiers. So they had to consider this carefully but would be in touch.

Hello. I trust you've left the DVD with Badbakht's secretary, *magnifique, merci monsieur*. Very good nice, as they say. And say hello to Mina thank you. Please do not forget to wear the Zahedan three-piece, I was going to mention something about that but cannot remember what. And FYI check out the link to the latest issue of the *Lufthansa Gazette*. Column entitled 'Things to Remember, Places to Go'. Kisses, S

Things to Remember, Places to Go! Starting spring 2002: The Promessa Gallery Tehran! The Promessa is a sexy arty gallery space right in the heart of the Islamic Republic, founded by curator Tirdad Zolghadr. For a time, people were worried Zolghadr might be a real fascist because he's known to wear military uniforms and lets himself be filmed walking around Tehran like a robot. And his exhibitions are always bold and orderly!! But Zolghadr adores living in a very multicultural corner of Tehran; he loves the diversity. That's not very fascist at all! He also donates money to AIDS/HIV+ charities. That's not very fascist either!! He just doesn't like 'pompous liberals', or 'elitism', and reacts against that. Zolghadr wants to be 'normal' in one sense – partly in order to get attention from people who wouldn't like 'wacky' curators – but then be subversive from within that position. He's not even really posh. He comes from an extremely modest background. His acquired poshness is just part of his surreal sexy art pose. And why not? We met Zolghadr in London just a year ago, after his talk at the Photographer's Gallery. As always he was very polite and kind and signed our leaflets ('with love from') very courteously and we couldn't think of anything to say to him – there was no point complimenting him because he must hear it all the time. Zolghadr is a committed promoter of young artists and seems to delight in so being. So maybe you can't even say he's part of an elite art world. Although he is. Zolghadr once said: 'I want the most accessible modern form with which to create the most modern speaking visual pictures of our time. My reason for curating exhibitions is to change people and not to congratulate them on being how they are.' A noble aim for any man to have! Daily flights Frankfurt > Tehran page 89.

A day later I'm woken by a telephone call from Badbakht's secretary. Mr Badbakht urgently wishes to see me regarding a minor and yet pressing detail. A signature on a photocopy that wasn't legible, and other minor matters, if only I could pass by the office this morning, or in the afternoon at the very latest, Mr Badbakht would gladly explain everything to me in person. As a matter of fact, I cannot remember this particular secretary of Badbakht's, a woman with a surprisingly husky voice, sounding much like the color-blind Zahedan transvestite with the skin disease who is to paint the SACs, and for a moment I wonder whether this isn't a prank on his part, or Stella's.

I take a cab to the Ministry the next day, but after walking up and down the aisles for nearly half an hour I still cannot seem to spot the right office, and when I ask a bored recruit on guard duty, stationed next to a water fountain on the second floor, he claims that Badbakht was actually transferred to a new post in Isfahan sometime last year. When I insist I was summoned by Badbakht only yesterday, the recruit smiles warm-heartedly, shrugs his shoulders and says it really isn't his problem in the first place.

Sitting in Mr Kambakhsh's office an hour later, a tulip-shaped clock and standard A4 color photocopies of the Revolutionary Leaders on the wall, Kambakhsh calmly explains that, needless to say, the recruit must have been referring to some other Mr Badbakht. Perhaps. For Kambakhsh could indeed vaguely remember two colleagues from the accounts department being transferred to Abadan last March, indeed, but as for the Mr Badbakht I had recently met, actually, incidentally, he, too, had left his post here at the Ministry of Culture, it was all very unexpected and unfortunate, just last night. A case of some embarrassing, some very embarrassing material found in his drawer. But in any case, he was not in a position to speak about the events here at the Ministry, which, needless to say, always touched on some question of national security or other. And that aside, there was the privacy of Mr Badbakht's family relatives to take into account, poor fellow, may God be merciful upon him.

'By the way, some are saying that at one point you handed Mr Badbakht a file, you see, on, well, on a video CD I believe it was. Or a DVD, perhaps?'

'A DVD.'

'Well, that makes sense, in a way. For it is actually precisely what Mr Badbakht was saying. He was saying you hadn't handed him anything at all. But be that as it may, and quite needless to say, it's pretty obvious you didn't. How could you have gotten into his drawer if it was double-locked, right? Luckily for us, we had a spare key. But you see, sir, people like the honorable Mr Tarofi, they really want the best for you. Contrary to the other riffraff you associate with. You see, we're still waiting for a gesture of good faith on your part. Something assuring us of your honesty and good intentions. Needless to say, it really needn't be something we couldn't do ourselves, just a personal gesture of some kind. I'm sure you know what I'm getting at.'

'A gesture of good faith on my part.'

'I think you do know what we're getting at. After all, you did grant us your signature.'

'I wasn't aware it had anything to do with the Ministry.'

'Be that as it may.'

I decide to nod, grimly and knowingly.

As I'm leaving the Ministry, Zsa Zsa calls from Karaj, suggesting I drop by for a party that very evening. The cultural attaché of the Chinese embassy is attending, 'a cultivated man well known for his generous support for local cultural events', particularly in the field of tribal arts and local handicrafts.

I switch on the portable TV, first to Balkan Bang, just long enough to see another horse carriage occurrence in the old parts of Prague, though with different actors, then switch through several local channels. I eventually sit down to watch a half-hour amateur documentary on a wedding ceremony somewhere in Zimbabwe. At several moments during the film one sees elephants, gazelles and giraffes standing nearby, looking as if they were witnessing the ceremony from within the bushes. It's already dark by the time the film ends.

The plumbing chirps at me as I shower. I take ten minutes to choose a shirt to go with the three-piece suit, then put on Puma running shoes and call a cab. Just before leaving the apartment I change into another shirt.

In the taxi towards Karaj I roll down the window, light a cigarette and consider the chances of Mehrangiz being at the party, soon finding myself rehearsing familiar fantasies regarding her wide hips and ample thighs, her buttocks and shoulder blades. I flick cigarette ash off my sleeve and try to think of something else.

I'm wearing what is actually my favorite three-piece, with generous seventies lapels and thick stripes of light brown and dark gold. I found the suit in Zahedan, in a thrift store in an industrial warehouse. The entire front section of the warehouse was filled with clothes donated by the International Red Cross. The back, where I bought a nineteenth-century handcrafted milking stool, contained antique jewelry, antique doorways and artful wooden furniture. These had been looted from abandoned Afghani households, or hastily sold by the fleeing owners to middlemen with contacts in Zahedan, where other middlemen shipped them to feel-good ethnic art fairs in New York.

Zsa Zsa's living-room is a den of peaked doorways, whitewashed walls, embroidered pillows, Qashqai carpets and an enormous brick fireplace. Playing in the background is Portishead and the NY Philharmonic. Live in Roseland. I help myself to pistachios, sliced celery, olives in ground pomegranate and potato chips with garlic yogurt. *The blackness of darkness forever*, says Portishead.

On the dinner table near the hearth I notice the cultural pages of a reformist daily, where someone has highlighted an editorial on Mehrangiz's upcoming show at the Italian pavilion in Venice. Her piece, according to the cautiously critical editor, was a seven-minute loop called 'Forced Marriage', showing seven bearded men in collarless white shirts, chanting war slogans and chasing seven veiled figures up and down sand dunes. The piece was filmed in the Sonoran Desert.

As I walk out into the garden, I can see Zsa Zsa and Cyrus sitting by the far end of the swimming pool with their backs to the house, between them a young woman whom I only recognize as I draw closer, thanks to the sweet, musky smell of Chloë. The moment Mina sees me she starts patiently searching her leather satchel for some visibly indispensable object or other.

Aside from two thumb rings and several dozen silver bracelets up and down her arms, Mina has a pair of Oakley sunglasses suspended from her ears, dangling below her chin in a manner now fashionable throughout Tehran, both north and south. Seated next to her, Zsa Zsa, in her customary corduroys and checked shirt, is in an unusually talkative mood, telling favorite anecdotes from her student days, the larks and capers in thirties Paris, when she discovered how to withdraw considerable amounts of money from local banks by using alternating account numbers and surnames.

'So this was how I paid for my university tuition, my nightlife, my cocaine and, later on, even for a car, even though I never owned a driver's licence in my life, I mean I never needed one at the Legion,' she says, wagging her ivory walking cane. 'And so one night, it must have been the fifties, this copper, *ce flic*, he asks for my driver's licence, and I'm thinking oh hell what now. So

I just show my Iranian birth certificate and say I'm really sorry everything's written in Farsi.'

'Well done.'

'Yes, but the thing is, now there's this stamp in the middle of my birth certificate saying "This driver's licence is hereby endorsed for six months".'

With Mina still furiously exploring her satchel, I nervously shuffle back to the house in the dark, towards the grandiloquent sounds of Portishead in Roseland. I can make out Zsa Zsa's voice at the other end of the garden, launching into the story of getting arrested for espionage by Column 2, because of her dirty pimp bastard scumbag boss, such a dirty pimp bastard scumbag that guy was.

I find myself watching San, once again, as she stands in a far corner of the room, two feet taller than the students crowding around her politely insisting that she relate absolutely everything she knows about the European reception of Hafez.

'Which translations do they use?'

'I have no fucking idea.'

'Does anyone read the originals?'

'Most probably not.'

Most of Zsa Zsa's guests have gathered around the Chinese cultural attaché, who is casually leaning against a wall. 'So I do this article on Iranian economic policy, saying, well, it's basically very simple. Big difference between China and Iran is Iran thinks it can do political reform without economic reform. How can you have political reform without economic reform? In China, first we do economic reform, then do political reform, then we check. Was this political reform good or bad for economic reform? Anyway my article is, well, you know, diplomatically written, or at least that's what I thought.' He shrugs, takes a swig from his Carlsberg. 'But then this friend calls me up. He says, congratulations Salman! I say what do you mean? My name isn't Salman. Who the fuck is Salman? So he says, well, Keyhan newspaper quoted you in the little blue box on the first page, and that blue box on the first page of Keyhan, well, what it amounts to actually is a kind of hit list. That's where they put people they don't like. In the little blue box. So I go, so what? Fuck them, you know? Who the fuck cares?'

'Guy speaks amazing Farsi,' someone mutters. 'Incredible. Where did you learn Farsi?'

I was once in the blue Keyhan box myself, after writing an article on a food orgy here at Zsa Zsa's. I wait for a cue, a chance to bring this up, but the conversation is moving too quickly. 'I didn't think a Chinese would ever bother to learn Farsi.'

'Actually', the diplomat continues, 'China and Iran have lots in common, you know. In modern times, China and Iran have had more revolutions than any other country worldwide. Simultaneous mass rebellions in different urban centers.'

'Accent is perfect.'

'Yes, but he doesn't pronounce the "q"s, did you notice, he pronounces them like a "k" almost.'

'And this is because Iran had a sense of belonging way back, before modern times, just like China. And neither China nor Iran had much Western influence. Much less than Arab countries. And much less than, you know, India or whatever.'

Cyrus is standing next to me, one hand firmly gripping my shoulder, trying to spark a casual conversation on the women attending the party, see the one with the lip-job and the enormous ass, in the black jeans, she reminds me of the first woman I ever slept with *vallah beh khoda*, but bonding with Cyrus does not come naturally with Mina in the background, and I'm overjoyed to see San from the corner of my eye, walking up to us as she lights a cigarette. Without bothering to comment on the ass and the lip-job, I take a tiny step sideways, so as to encourage San to step up, though not obviously enough for Cyrus to notice.

'The Iranian student intelligentsia. Our pride and joy. Amazing. A-ma-zing. How can you lead a country to cultural enlightenment if you don't know how to eat a fucking pastry without meat crumbs sticking to your face? How can you do that without knowing how to match the fucking colors of your fucking suit? Amazing.' San is oblivious to Cyrus's irritated glare. She finishes lighting the cigarette with her left hand, pocketing a wallet and holding a meat pastry in the other, and in her characteristic mumble she starts describing a press conference she attended that day, just hours before, at the Tehran Museum of Modern Art.

'So there's a press conference at the Museum. OK. We're this select group of international correspondents, the usual suspects, actually. None of us knows exactly why we've been convoked. But OK. Then what happens? This guy gets on stage and presents us with – get this – with a collection of Adolf Hitler's watercolors. I'm serious. The Führer's watercolors. In: Tehran. Talk about an Aryan connection. And those Ministry officials make no fucking attempt to explain why these particular pieces of artwork just happen to be lying in the fucking cellar all these years. I mean really. They simply shuffle around the fucking podium,' she imitates the officials, stooping over and wagging her head as if imitating some demented primate, 'scratching their stubble, looking slightly embarrassed and carry the damn things back down into the cellar again. I swear.'

Cyrus has started walking away, towards the Beijing diplomat, who is now fiddling with a turquoise chain of tasbi prayer beads. Scrutinizing San as she absent-mindedly watches the guests in the middle of the room, most of them dancing to some pre-revolutionary Googoosh track with a Cha-Cha-Cha rhythm, I still cannot quite decide whether to find her attractive or not. Cheekbones perfectly molded, the eyes an exotic green, but unfortunately a touch too tall and too slender, and her mouth, I find, is simply enormous, and her breasts by far too small.

'You know, San, my dear,' I lower my voice to a conspiring and intimate murmur, 'that Adolf retrospective may have been the best local show in a long, long time.' San shrugs and raises her eyebrows in a 'Truth Hurts What Can I Say?' demeanor.

'Yes, truth hurts, what can I say? But something else. You know what?' San leans over, her voice now equally conspiring. 'I heard that bastard Tarofi is now involved in something dicey. And I don't mean his good-goody reformism and all that. Something big. Something about armed opposition outside and inside the country and espionage and counter-espionage and counter-fucking-counter-espionage and so-called terrorist fucking networks and God knows what the fuck else. To me, the whole thing seems to be a mess. A complete and utter mess. Which is of course typical. Just fucking typical. How can you run a country if you can't even run a fucking secret service properly?'

'You're so right.' I light a cigarette and take a sip from my drink.

'Sounds like utter chaos. Tell me how on earth did you find out?'

'This guy from the Cultural Ministry. Badback or something, his name is. But now I've been trying to reach him, and I don't know where the fuck he is. And I wanted to ask you whether you might know? I mean I'm sure you've been to the Ministry before? Badback or something? This new radical *Mani Pulite* guy they're all worried about?'

'Of course I know him, I mean I've heard of him before. Let me see what I can do.' I finish my drink and immediately start mixing another one. 'I'll ask around for you.'

'Anyway, usually, the Ministry of Information, it's always one step behind, even if it's always pretending it knows what's going on, just blindly hoping and praying someone will fill them in at some point, so I don't know how viable all of this is, but anyway, apparently, you have this Tarofi guy, who's completely broke, can't even buy a fucking precision spray pump for his fucking fruit trees, and who will work with anyone for anyone against anyone under anyone as long as the pay is OK. So he hooks up with these weirdo internationals, these networkers who, well, God knows what they're about, seem to run on sheer force of habit, on sheer downhill momentum, like the free-market economy, or the ecosystem or something, I mean they're filthy rich so it can't be the money, right? And they're not really leftist, and not really religious and not really this and not really that, maybe they're mercenaries after all, but there seems to be more, you know, some latest design in terms of wacko schmacko ideologues, something different, stuff for future headlines to come – or maybe they've been pulling strings all along, you know? Don't you think?'

I noisily finish a second drink, put an arm around San's waist and burp, emitting a strong smell of olives, vinegar and fennel. She looks at me with concern, as if I were an excretion of a particular, worrying hue she'd never expect to discover in her stool, then carefully rearranges her knee-length grey dress as she walks to the dance floor.

By 2 AM, I'm feeling light-headed due to the homemade raisin liquor and Parsi Cola, and have shared several lines of coke with Cyrus, which have had no effect whatsoever, and am now stumbling across the Qashqai carpet looking for more olives and fennel in grape vinegar. My fingers are sticky and reek of garlic yogurt, so I wipe them off on various tablecloths, where they leave greasy pink traces. Someone has finally replaced the Googoosh album with an early Enrique Iglesias, and Cyrus is dancing with a group of women I've never seen before. *Don't know why why but I love to see you cry*, says Iglesias. *Don't know why why it just makes me feel alive.* The Chinese cultural attaché is still standing precisely where he was two hours ago but is now talking to Mina. I walk towards them, reaching for more olives, pistachios and fennel as I make my way across the room and try very hard to understand what they're saying, but the music is simply too loud. When the track finally ends I lean over and mutter into the diplomat's ear.

'So Mr Ching Chong Hong Kong, looking a little uptight, you know. Just don't be afraid to use adjectives when you talk to women.' The cultural attaché nods a curt goodbye and walks off, leaving me standing alone with Mina, who smiles politely before following the diplomat to the far end of the room. I reach over and swab off my fingers on her back.

After mixing another drink of vodka with fresh lime, I stumble across the room until I'm standing in the middle of the dancers, then use my forefingers to pull my eyes into little slits, screaming '*Spwing Woll, Stuh Fwy*' at the top of my lungs, until most guests make their way to the outside veranda, for a breath of fresh air.

Hearsay

Our hotel is near Chinatown. You know they say the Chinese in London have the same lifestyles as the Chinese in China. They hang glistening orange ducks in their shop windows and what goes on in those shops I do not know. Do not want to know. I just know it stinks. When you pass by those shops in hot weather it stinks so bad I feel like throwing up. It smells of sweet, rotting fish. Each and every time I pass by in front of a Chinese shop I feel like throwing up on the sidewalk. But I still want to go and check out Chinatown every day, even if it makes me want to throw up. As for the Promessa, I talked to my Ideal Standard associate whom you know, he was the one telling you all that crap about the Kabbalists back at the gay bar in Hamburg (His name's Türgüt, and he keeps saying I have 'a love/hate relationship' with the Chinese ...!) We were happy to meet you, by the way. It would have been a boring evening otherwise, and we worked out something pretty good. But we were wondering if you could reconsider the title. Because we're considering using Jordi Grotesk as a font. On a yellow and red, combat color background. But Promessa ends with an A. And has precisely eight letters. So it doesn't work out, graphically speaking, even a word with nine letters would be better. How about 'Promesses' in French? Which is promises, the plural. Or in English? Cyrus tells me promise in Farsi is 'koskesh', which is cool, too. Why not call it that? And why is it in Italian anyway? And so yes I actually met Cyrus Rahati at a party last week. He said you kept trying to fuck his girlfriend but she didn't want you. Isn't that funny – such a small world. Thanks and email us back as soon as you can. Yours, Fatih.

PS: You know what happened: I was looking through dv film material I shot in Hamburg and suddenly found that I shot you somewhere in the streets there. Funny, don't you think? I did not expect to see anyone that I knew in Hamburg.

I also have an email from the office assistant at the I-CON, saying they've decided to fund the project, after all, on condition that I present it at a conference on 'Spaces of Global Art' next June. I'd need to package the Promessa as 'an exercise in artistic cartography, an interdisciplinary project for mapping a transfer of contemporary forms of knowledge across theoretical-practical and ethno-geographic boundaries'. Considering that the opening is only weeks away, I should drop by in Zurich as soon as possible.

Stella's email, finally, is unusually brief, stating only that, according to the international press, a *Newsweek* correspondent had fallen off the roof of an office building near Karaj last night, but that it wasn't considered a suicide by the authorities. She had not left a note of any kind, and the multiple fractures in each of the fingers of her right hand had apparently occurred before her hapless fall from the rooftop.

I feel a peculiar tension in my lower abdomen. Pulling the air deep into my gut, I switch off the computer and the portable TV, then pour myself a whiskey and walk over to the window, where I watch the rush-hour traffic on the freeway. The cars are barely moving, bumper to bumper in a seamless succession of tinny metal roofs reflecting the beam of the streetlights, a blinding white glare with just a hue of dark orange along the rim.

The next morning I wake with a splitting headache, and decide to grab some air before breakfast. In the courtyard downstairs, I notice some new graffiti in English, CAN I FUCK YOU IN THE NIGHT, sprayed in extravagant capital letters across the entrance patio of block 30B. I spend an hour in the glaring afternoon sunshine by the soccer pitch, where a group of teenagers are kicking a football back and forth across the field, peacefully and amicably, and agreeably boring to watch. On the far side of a dusty expanse of unused land, framed by the fumy, gray-white skies above, and the eight-lane freeway at their feet, I count sixteen slabs of Korean make, each of them twenty stories high and six apartments wide. Halfway across the unused field, nestled into a small slope by the freeway, is the *bassiji* bungalow simmering in the early summer heat. I decide to inquire about the DV camera within the next two days.

I spend the rest of the day at home, seeing as I cannot think any more clearly than before my walk. Today's hangover is patently much worse than anything I can remember, even the splitting headache following the housewarming party a month ago, during which, as I now rather painfully remember, I made several drunken passes at San, who tactfully ignored me each and every time. At one point, I now recall, I even made a comment on the size of San's mouth and its potential advantages in terms of group sex and male anatomies and such, which is when she and most of the other guests started thanking me for the party and taking off for a late birthday dinner somewhere else.

I'm about to take another shower when, from my bathroom window, I notice a sudden change in the apartment opposite. Sitting on the Louis XV sofas and armchairs in the usually deserted living room is a family of six having afternoon *chaii*. I can barely distinguish their outlines through the tinted windows, but I can make out a small girl of four or five years of age, taking pictures of her relatives with a flashing Polaroid. She shows each snapshot to an elderly woman by the window, who never fails to applaud enthusiastically.

So we've received your description of the Promessa project, thank you very much. It would be wise to get on with things as soon as possible. Please book a flight to Zurich, see to it that you coordinate things with the assistant. Just one thing. It seems to me that in your Promessa statement, you're implying 'art' doesn't really play the role it should in Iran, or anywhere else in the Middle East. Well, for one thing, to pretend it should exist in the same form it does anywhere else – now that is truly colonialist. The 'hybrid' or 'postcolonial' horse hockey you see in European museums has precious little to do with typical living conditions in the Third World. People in places like Black Africa find the act of staring at pictures on a wall extremely boring, just as they find staring at lines on a page, alone in some corner of the room, very odd. Why should it be incorrect or insulting to point these things out? I look forward to a frank and genuine debate on such matters, which are, indeed, of great importance to me. Sincerely, Dr T. Christenhuber.

I turn on the TV, switching to CNN, light a cigarette and mix a date vodka with generous amounts of lime and Zam Zam Cola.

Dearest Tan, my old friend. Millions of Tehran households have Rembrandt, Van Gogh, Dali or Miro posters, or Persian miniatures, or Islamic knick-knacks on their kitchen walls. So much for a lack of art. Then again, who cares? If art touches on grassroots, terrific. But to be frank and genuine, for that we have World Music Festivals and *Terre des hommes*.

Roughly half an hour later, there's a brief glitch in the power supply, and the text is lost. Furious, I start pounding my hand-crafted Afghan milking stool against the wall, then throw it out the living-room window, watching it land in the courtyard, very near the spot where my notebook must have landed two weeks ago. I take the elevator down to the ground floor, pick up the stool, which is still intact, and return to the apartment for another drink.

Several months ago I had a black-and-white portrait of Zsa Zsa blown up to life-size for the new Promessa. Zsa Zsa with her hair in a beehive, wearing a thick woolen jacket with swirling sixties motifs, her expression stern and deadpan, arms folded, an unlit cigarette in one hand. I had it framed and hung by the entrance, at the beginning of the winding hallway, where the zebra stripes are being painted over by one of the Afghanis, who have now been dressed in matching mauve uniforms.

Recently Zsa Zsa announced that she did have the intention of attending the vernissage, even though it would be hard on her. 'So many memories, my dear.' Memories aside, I know Zsa Zsa would disapprove of seeing her picture suspended in a public corridor, like some political portrait or Parsi Cola poster board, and very much hope she'll change her mind. I think it will be quite an experience, for more reasons than one.

Since the catering, the soft drinks, the espresso machines, the chandeliers, the ashtrays, the Ecusson chairs, the lounge chairs and the terrarium are all in place, the opening has been set for precisely two weeks from now. I'm considering the option of inviting the young man with the 'Sleep of a Thousand Destinies' piece from the Conceptual Art Festival and placing him, equipped with his bedspread and his mirror, at the symmetric center of the gallery space. At a well-chosen moment during the evening, I would put an arm around him in a tender gesture of affection, upon which, perhaps without even lifting the sheet, I could introduce him to the crowd. The perfect posture for a welcome speech, an inaugural talk, expressing my thoughts and impressions, hopes and doubts regarding the Promessa, the artworld, and of course my own, deeply problematic, Westernized mindset. On how naive it had been to try and find in Tehran what I'd come to see as quality over in the West.

I would then scorn and chastise the *Euroamerican Weltbild*, the fallacy of patiently waiting for capitalism to make its way around the world, spawning plenty of good art in its wake, the arrogant assumption that places not yet subsumed under the logic of Capital would simply join the others in time, like latecomers at a dinner party. Holding the young artist to my side, actually smiling down at him benignly, perhaps clutching his hand from underneath the bedspread, I would say it was up to him, him and his *compagnons de route*, to undermine the Hegelian dynamic. To incapacitate the conceit of a historiography serving only to prove its own logic. To expose the phantasmagoria of an emancipatory Spirit of Global Capitalism.

The *bassiji* officer has finally sent me a tape, along with the camera, thanking me profusely, mentioning that his sister-in-law had taken the Panasonic to a wedding ceremony in Shahr-e Rey and that the results were simply marvelous. The thank-you note ends with two stanzas from a Hafez poem, Farsi at its most impenetrable, something to do with drunken dervishes and the futility of life.

The first half-hour of the DV tape shows teenage *bassijis* waving at the trembling, unfocussed camera, cracking jokes, reciting more stanzas from eleventh-century poetry, including, incidentally, some early Kalegondeh, and greeting their friends and families as if they were on nationwide TV. Maman, I miss you so much, really I do. You gave me everything, I'd be nothing without you, Maman. But the remaining hour on the tape shows a quiet walk through the City Park, an off-voice commenting on the beauty of Iranian trees, the splendor of the Iranian mountainside and the long hiking sprees of the Iranian youth, who trek through the Alborz mountains as if it were a necessity, a matter of life and death, but who are actually walking out of sheer love for nature.

You can find so much truth in the Iranian people's love for nature. So much truth.

I edit a six-minute episode from the City Park sequence, saturate the colors and decide to present it at the opening as a collective work-in-progress by the Zirzamin Militia, calling it '*Magiciens de la terre*'. Moreover, the color-blind Zahedani has already started painting the first SAC items on to canvas, and both the crime novelist and the Baltimore Muslim have confirmed their readings, although Stella, on the other hand, has cancelled hers.

> Sorry I can't. We can discuss when you come to Zurich, book flight tomorrow morning. Promessa sounds toptabulosa. I hear even celebrities are coming your way. Have you heard the Neil Diamond rumor? He was last in China. Too bad about San. Just wish you would check back with us before you act from time to time. Read a new novel the other day, a very nice saga-esque submission from Uruguay. The writer said it was a tale of 'poverty through poverty via poverty back to poverty'. More anon. Off to buy a coffee from the cute/scary Albanians downstairs. GeStella PS I was going to say something about the purple pizzeria bathroom tiles and the bit with the architects in the Prada dinner jackets under 'Patronage', remind me when we meet.

Due to a deep and pious sense of faith in the metaphysics of Helvetic safety standards, throughout my childhood, my parents would invariably fly Swissair, and the flights on Swissair aircraft gradually became an unchanging, cherished childhood memory. A *Heimatgefühl* enmeshed with the luscious aura of privilege, embedded in a carefully composed symbolic universe. The adorable little cross on the tailfin, the marine-blue vomit bags, the comic-strip emergency regulations, the Cailler chocolate before landing, the sturdy women and tender men in ink-blue uniforms, cautioning and thanking the passengers in the many marvelous accents of the *Confédération Helvétique.*

Any country of such tiny size as Switzerland, packed with as many communes and cantons, national languages, celebrated design traditions, petty regional contentions and government parties in power would indeed be the perfect starting point for any modern sense of national habitat. As liberating as it is synthetic, a product of historical circumstance and meticulous risk management, rather than any deep-seated emotional consensus. Sitting next to me on the Tehran–Zurich flight is an elderly couple talking in a Swiss-German dialect I cannot understand, although I can make out the terms 'Shiraz' and 'beautiful prostitutes'.

'*Moll, Shiraz isch huara-schön gsii. Chash nüd sägä.*' Both of them are wearing baseball caps, Nike sneakers and Michel Jordi wristwatches.

As the plane takes off from Mehrabad airport, I start flicking through a notebook bearing a daisy-shaped sticker of the Revolutionary Leader on the cover. Zsa Zsa, letter to Rock Hudson, Regal Springs Cruise Ship 1976. No one here speaks any English, but that's OK. I've used my hands before. I reach into my bag and pull out another notebook at random, but even before opening it I'm sidetracked by fantasies involving Stella and Mehrangiz, but also starring Mina and her charming chuckle, her dark eyes and slender fingers sloppily wiping my come off her Chevrolet dashboard.

The aircraft wheels up to the arrival gate, past a billboard saying, '*Grüezi!* Welcome to Unique!' in Tyler Brûlé polish. Muzak by the Alan Parsons Project starts piping at the passengers from above their seats. As I'd half suspected, Stella isn't there to meet me at Unique Grüezi Airport, merely sending a string of lengthy text messages.

Her numerous attempts to reach me on my cellphone had failed, she says, 'for as we all know, Iran has an operating network that stops at its national borders, as in the Zoroastrian precept of a territorial God'. Stella does, however, confirm that Dr Christenhuber would have time to meet me at the I-CON in person, but would also be arriving in Tehran on the night of the opening, towards 1 AM. 'He's really looking forward to this.'

She then describes the way to the apartment by taxi, leaving a key at the information desk, in a small manila envelope, and recommending 'early-morning jogging and sunbathing on the Seefeld side of the lake, the aubergine appetizer at the Darius, the Sashimi at the Hopp Sushi near the station, the Komplett Bar by the Limmat, and this spooky Shiite brotherhood thing on the Förrlibuckstrasse, might interest you, who knows'. She also mentions her local dealer Marco 'for anything you might need by way of uppers or downers or whatever.'

The cab driver is a young Tamil with an immature, fluffy moustache, his radio tuned to a station playing one hard rock evergreen after another. *Gina dreams of running away, when she cries in the night, Tommy whispers baby it's OK, someday.* After a ten-minute drive, we reach a residential area where almost everyone, as far as I can see, is wearing a bulky DJ bag and a pair of plastic flip-flops, neo-Celtic designs tattooed up and down their arms. We come to a halt in front of a high-rise apartment building just behind a soccer stadium, from where I can make out the happy sounds of a Metallica concert.

After stopping the car, the driver gently places a ringed forefinger on the digital display, indicating a sum that would have caused Mehrangiz to bargain for a good hour and a half. But I, with my usual, capricious meandering between blushing courtesy and an aggressive display of indifference, which some, particularly the Francophone, tend to consider mysterious and attractive, even thank the cab driver as I clumsily duck my head to step out of the car.

The furniture in Stella's thirty-fourth floor apartment is unexpectedly plain. An Ikea sofabed, a silk Chinese carpet, two potted lemon trees placed on either side of the balcony. By the doorway are several shelves filled entirely with stiletto shoes, with an additional shelf for high-heeled boots of black or white leather.

From the balcony I can see the lake and city center surrounded by a small expanse of dark green hills nestled around the lake of Zurich, bathed in a spectacular sunset of red, scarlet and cherry blue. Just next to Stella's apartment building are three other towers, of precisely the same build and height. I count the balconies of the tower opposite, every single one perfectly empty save for flowerpots, or tables and chairs of white plastic. I light a cigarette, then change my mind and flick it over the railing before walking back inside to look through Stella's belongings. In the drawers of a tiny dressing-table in the bedroom I find a strap-on vibrator, some L'Oréal make-up, Pokémon corn snacks and several stacks of personal photographs, mostly of small children, Labradors, Boxers, German Shepherds and family relatives from Munich.

The refrigerator is empty save for *yakisoba* noodles, pickled shoga ginger, two open packs of Pokémon corn snacks and an untouched pack of Haribo *Gummibärchen*. A perfect set of props, straight out of nineties lifestyle journalism as written by young generations of bourgeois bohemians with studied routines, born of a vague sense of being told they were something special, if anxiously suspecting they were not. I realize I cannot see any books in the apartment, only a photocopied article on Marcus Garvey and one on Vincent Gallo, both in German.

I find a small collection of VHS tapes behind a cheap Grundig TV with a built-in VCR, and choose some seventies Italian softcore, but the video recorder jams, clicking and buzzing, and proceeds to chew up the cassette. I extract it from the VCR with the help of a fork and a pair of scissors and insert another tape, labeled *Foot Fetish Interracial*, then another, *Sinnliche Rebellen: Vincent Gallo*, and a third, *Sinnliche Rebellen: Dr Boris Groys*. Which are all, in turn, destroyed by the VCR as it reduces smooth, luminous tape to crinkled filament. Although I'm not looking forward to seeing Uncle Tan in the slightest, I call the I-CON nonetheless, to hear a recorded announcement thanking the caller for calling but not allowing for a message of his own.

The next morning, upon hearing the same message on the I-CON answering machine, I decide to drop by unannounced. It's raining as the driver stops in front of a massive steel door in bright yellow, I-CON spelled out in fluorescent orange in the upper right-hand corner. I walk up to the entrance and notice a camera lens at eye level, just above the buzzer. I press it, sheepishly eyeing the lens, and the door clicks open almost instantly. Once inside, I scrutinize the door and realize the lens is a fake, the surveillance camera a cheap piece of fiction, precisely the kind of affected prank that longtime academics would indulge in.

I walk down an unlit corridor, along a series of empty rooms, all equipped with spacious office desks with unusually glossy black desktops, until I reach a small foyer, where I'm received by a tubby brunette in high heels, a tight skirt and a black denim shirt that goes well with her unsparing bust, impish, dark eyes and blushing cheeks. Very much reminiscent of the fuck-me cheeks and the big eyes, or was it vice versa.

'*Der Herr* Doktor Christenhuber', she announces, was at a biweekly fundraising meeting with Business Unusual, the board of official sponsors of AVANTI, a federal committee charged with 'catalyzing creative approaches to stimulating the national economy', but he would probably be here in a few minutes. She leaves me to study the I-CON brochures announcing upcoming events and publications and wondering whether the Promessa would fit in among these studied contemplations of amputee video artists, Polish postmodernism, Saigon urban design, oral histories of Peruvian head massage, black-market trade routes in Albania and Greece, and Mapping Hetereologia: Liminality and the Everyday Cultures of Shanghai.

Within half an hour or so, Christenhuber is walking in to greet me, one arm eagerly outstretched to shake my hand, wearing his felt hat and black corduroys, a black cashmere sweater casually thrown over his shoulders. He offers me espresso in the meeting room, where the conference table has the same peculiar, plastic surface I noticed in the remaining rooms along the hall. As I sit down, I realize the surface reflects the moisture from my palms in the form of two prominently glistening sweat patches, with several smaller ones where my fingertips were.

Tan, familiar with the furniture and its disciplinary potentialities, grips the rim of his espresso cup with one hand, the other resting on his right forearm, making little drumming motions with his fingers. When I mention the camera lens downstairs, he throws back his head and chortles loudly at the ceiling without interrupting the thrum of his fingers on his arm, as if I'd mentioned an old, private joke between the two of us. Going back to some essay, say, by Donna Haraway or Trinh T. Minh-ha. I hopefully assume that, following my fit at the Restaurant Central, the air is cleared between us once again. Christenhuber gathers himself, interrupting the drumming of his fingers only to wipe a tear out of the corner of his eye, the other hand still gripping his cup, then enquires about my position on African art, on the Promessa and on Tarofi's projects for the local art scene.

After a brief chat on recent happenings in Tehran, including the unfortunate loss of San, and a second espresso that was brought in by the assistant, Christenhuber eventually concludes that, if I don't mind his saying so, I don't seem to have much personal distance from the subject matter as a whole, and whether I think this might hinder or otherwise affect my sense of critical analysis. I savor thick waves of pristine rage surging up through my gut and lapping at my temples. But remembering the many contracts and obligations, promises and pledges I have made in Tehran and elsewhere, I briefly close my eyes, fighting the urge to ask for the restrooms and leave the building as discreetly as I can, obediently answering that no, no I think not, you can rest assured on that count.

For lack of a better idea, I take a cab to what Stella referred to as the 'Komplett Bar'. Sitting on a barstool by the Limmat river, I find myself surrounded by slender men and women in their twenties and thirties, all in tasteful flip-flops, drinking light beers from transparent plastic cups, smoking a brand called Parisienne Mild. Most are tattooed. A woman in Ray Ban sunglasses and camouflage flip-flops brushes past, swirling, neo-Celtic symbolics on her lower back, stretching down to her buttocks beneath her blue jeans, and I'm reminded of the Japanese tattoo artist on the BBC.

'Bootkick Here,' I speculate. 'Please Insert Celtic Blowhorn Here'.

Seated at the other end of the bar, I notice the I-CON office assistant with the Persian cheeks, sipping on peach daiquiri and reading a paperback, a large DJ bag lying nearby. I watch her as she drinks, immersed in her paperback, occasionally lighting a Parisienne Mild or rearranging the slush in her daiquiri with her straw, her dark-brown hair tied back into a bun, wearing designer camouflage fatigues and a white T-shirt with BRITNEY SWALLOWS stenciled across the front. I slide off the barstool and walk over to her, trying to breathe the air all the way down into my lower gut. I can now see she has a small Celtic pattern on her forearm and is reading Marguerite Duras.

'Excuse me.' She looks up from *Les petits chevaux de Tarquinia*. 'Have you had dinner?'

'I suppose I know you from somewhere?' She grimly shuts her Duras paperback, though not without positioning a cardboard bookmark at the appropriate page.

'No. I don't think so.' I hesitate. 'I mean, yes. You do. We met this morning at the I-CON. Have you had dinner?'

She orders the green chicken curry, I have a papaya salad and determine that her boyfriend owns a futon store, that she's finished her studies in New Interaction Design at the Art Academy, that she's working part-time at the I-CON and that she just got back from Cadiz where she was taking a winter course in beginner's Spanish. When she asks me my name, I thank God it isn't Franz or Michael, for it always offers a good ten minutes' worth of conversation. 'Khatami: sounds like a futon, doesn't it?' I quip, which makes her giggle.

She asks me a series of questions on Tehran, and Iran, but also on the pan-Arab movement, and on Arab women's rights, and the cultural politics of the Arab mass media in the Arab world. Rather than point out the standard geocultural inaccuracy, I do my best to answer. Nasser, Queen Rania, Al-Jazeera, and after another ten minutes of conversation I ask her whether she'd like to go home with me.

'Don't think so,' she says, 'I really don't think so.'

We smile sheepishly, first at each other, then down at our plates. I take off my glasses, clean them with my shirtsleeve and put them on again. Twenty feet away, a woman in tight blue jeans and a studded leather belt is twirling a little girl around, both of them laughing and giggling. Watching them from a wooden cot nearby is a man in camouflage shorts and a white T-Shirt saying

PUNK'S NOT DEAD in ransom note cutouts, a plastic beer glass in one hand. I'm wondering whether to try and convince her to at least reconsider, or whether to simply walk away, when she stands up and thanks me for dinner. This is when I realize she has pockmarks around her chin and wonder why I hadn't noticed before.

'Time to get back to my *Petits chevaux de Tarquinia*.' She smiles sweetly at me.

'Guess so.' I do my best to smile back.

I stay where I am, watching long processions of tattooed men and women with perfect tans, immaculate pedicures and designer sunglasses. The man on the wooden cot, a persisting, dreamy smile on his lips, is still observing the forever twirling woman and spinning child, shrieking and chortling in the hazy sunset.

Someone taps me on the shoulder. It's the I-CON secretary, smiling down at me. 'I changed my mind,' she says, visibly only half convinced by her decision.

In the elevator to the thirty-fourth floor, I unbutton her army fatigues, stroking her nervously, then stick several fingers into her at a time, moving them quickly back and forth, which obviously whets her appetite, since she starts breathing heavily into my mouth. I try to concentrate on her fingers, reaching for my penis through the open zipper, but I'm annoyed by the distinct scent of chicken and green curry. 'You're panting down my throat.'

'I'm sorry. I'm only breathing.'

'No, you're panting.' Inside the apartment, she's distracted by the view from the balcony, murmuring something in Swiss-German I cannot decipher, *huarageil*, in various intonations, *huaraGEIL, HUarageil, hu-a-ra-geil.* I take her hand and walk her back inside, towards the living-room table. As I pull down her trousers and fluorescent pink panties, I'm reminded of what Cyrus once told me as we were discussing sex and women and relationships and such, sharing a packet of Golden Love Deluxe at some party at Zsa Zsa's. Once the underwear's off, it's jackpot time. The rest is afterthought.

I turn her around, and she bends over the table, propping herself up on her elbows. As I slip into her, I instantly feel I'm about to ejaculate, so I pull out again in an effort to postpone the inevitable, and awkwardly come between her thighs. I quickly pull up my jeans and Armani cotton underwear and hurry over to the toilet to get a Kleenex box, wishing she would leave. She smiles half-heartedly at me as she takes the tissues, but I don't smile back.

'Let's go for a beer,' I mutter. She looks relieved, nodding and buttoning her pants.

'Sure.' We stand side by side at the window for a moment, gazing down at the city, then I open the apartment door, letting her pass in front of me in a gesture of old-school courtesy. The moment she's outside, I slam the door shut and lock it behind her.

I wait for five seconds to go by, keeping perfectly still, then look through the spy-hole. She's standing outside, waving at me with a sarcastic, patronizing smile on her lips, then turns and makes for the elevator, shaking her head and rearranging her combat fatigues as she walks down the hall. I try to spot her at the foot of the building as she walks away, but then impatiently return to the living room to grab another VHS tape.

Later, in the elevator on my way down, I'm joined by a drug addict who smells of Fisherman's Friends and old sweat, wearing a light gray sweater saying, 'Have a Great 98'. She screams at the door in Swiss-German, alternately scratching two infected pimples on her brow, until the elevator reaches the second floor, where she leaves, wiping small traces of pus and blood on her sweater. I watch her lumber towards the fire escape, wondering whether she might potentially grace the Promessa entrance during the opening – 'Unique – Made in Switzerland' – but the door closes on me. I may have to ask Stella.

I step into the office of the Shiite Society on the ground floor of a light purple, postmodern office block in an industrial quarter of west Zurich, in the middle of an evening lecture. The room is covered in polyester flags of black, red and green, all with Farsi slogans, rallying cries, proverbs, logos, aphorisms, emblems and icons of Shiite bent and disposition. We Said YAA ALI, and Love Commenced.

I'm obliged by the friendly but insistent lecturer to sit down, don't feel uncomfortable, join the others, you're welcome here, my dear. So I clumsily take off my trainers and sit down on the thick Qashqai carpet with parallelogram patterns, next to a group of men in baggy blue jeans with innumerable zippers and buckles, sporting waxy hairstyles and the distinct smell of Paco Rabane. I can hear them occasionally mumble to each other in Arabic, which explains why the lecture is held not in Farsi but in graceless, faltering German. The rest of the audience consists of parents with small children on their laps, ostensibly Swiss women and their, to all appearances, Iranian husbands. They listen attentively to the lecturer as he ruminates on the theological pros and cons, the dos and don'ts of anti-Judaism, the men in jeans interrupting him every two minutes or so, inquiring, arguing and objecting, quoting the Qur'an in fluent Arabic.

As they leave the building after the lecture and the evening prayer, they check their phones for messages, then brutally yank their heads back and forth in different directions, loosening their neck muscles.

'Forget Zurich. What are you doing here anyway?' One of them asks me as he nestles a phone between his shoulder and his right ear, rolling up his shirtsleeves. 'I mean, we're talking Switzerland here, right? Which isn't even part of the European Union. It's a gap, a hole in the middle. Know what I'm saying.' He grins and offers a Barclays 100.

'Did you know the Swiss used to be mercenaries? All over Europe, all these kings and warlords used to hire these raging, screaming Swiss. That was the reputation, the Unique Selling Point. For centuries. And this, you know, at least this has some dignity if you think about it. Now: same nasty hostility, but without purpose. Just frustrated and furious in some weird way.' He focuses on his phone. 'Allu? Allu?'

Though sympathetic, I cannot take the angry young men very seriously, and decide they may be deliberately misleading me, for reasons I cannot know.

Walking towards Stella's apartment block, I look up to see that the lights are switched on, the windows forming a splendid row of small, bright rectangles against the night sky. I start running to the main door, slowing down as I reach the entrance, and pressing the elevator button as calmly as I can. On my way to the top floor my muscles contract in a shrill, jarring manner reminiscent of the first few hours in Shekufeh. As I step out into the corridor leading to the apartment, I pause once again, trying to breathe the air all the way down into my stomach.

Inside, the rooms are all dark. Everything in the apartment is precisely as I remember leaving it. Only the light bulbs are hot to the touch. I try to reach Stella, but her phone is switched off.

On the Swiss Airlines flight back to Tehran the inflight entertainment package offers a 'Punk Rock Retrospective', which includes not only Sammy Hagar, Boston and Oasis but also the Red Hot Chili Peppers, a band I find more revolting than ever, if only because it reminds me of my road trip with San. I try to concentrate on the notebooks but wind up listening to the Chili Pepper tracks from beginning to end, immersed and attentive.

I rarely turn away from what I find repugnant. I invariably stare, transfixed, every time I comes across magazine close-ups of medical anomalies, particularly those of acute skin diseases, of body parts covered in cysts, crusts and craters. In like fashion, I've never been able to resist the view of zoographic blowups of fleecy invertebrates devouring oozing insects. Or that of used Kleenex, white tennis socks, bushy armpits, bestiality, Bill Viola, Times New Roman font, or Che Guevara coffee mugs. Nor can I look away from newsreels of lethargic black Africans with houseflies crowding into the corners of their eyes and mouths.

The Swiss Airlines stewardess slowly approaches, row by row, with a tray of plastic cups of Coke and orange juice. I take off my headphones and wait, continuing the list of visual delicacies in my mind, both seductive and repugnant, charming and putrid. Greenpeace sympathizers, Bollywood aficionados, art deco shopping malls, pacifist bumper stickers, women who talk about their period, women with narrow hips, sports culture theorists, Central America, anal sex in hot weather.

'Coke or orange juice?' The stewardess looks very much like San, only shorter. I wonder why she's addressing me in English, despite my speaking to her in flawless German only minutes before, when I asked for an additional refreshing towel, and before that, as I was, incidentally, hesitating between the *Frankfurter Allgemeine* and *Die Neue Zürcher Zeitung*.

'*Orangensaft, danke, vielen Dank.*' When she returns with the food, I cannot help but clutch the *Neue Zürcher Zeitung* demonstratively in front of me, holding it aloft like courtly insignia at a medieval jousting spree. 'Chicken or fish, sir?'

'*Huhn oder Fisch? Huhn, danke.*'

Just before landing at Mehrabad airport, she asks me to 'please put your seat in the upright position, sir'. I ignore her and pretend to stare out the window at the vast, murky brine of blinking streetlights below. She reaches over to push the button on my armrest and yanks up the back of my seat without comment.

Opening

At home, I already have three messages from the I-CON secretary on the answering machine, insisting I phone the I-CON as soon as I can. I take a cold shower, check the tubes, pots and flasks by the sink, turn up the air-conditioning and dial the office number. The I-CON secretary answers the phone.

'Congratulations for what must have been an impressive project presentation,' she remarks. At first I cannot quite tell whether she's being sarcastic. 'Dr Christenhuber was impressed. But you do know, this is a scientific endeavor. To have enough critical distance, enough perspicacity, all that is key, you see. And you do realize you have to pull this through. You have a responsibility. Can't rely on us here to do the job for you. We're not Mummy and Daddy, you know.' The cinematic touch of the situation is not lost on me, and I smile as I reach for my cigarettes, enjoying the role of the impulsive stud who makes things hard for himself, the bumbling, martyred Casanova.

'So listen, Dr Christenhuber has looked through your file, and there are a couple of things you need to take care of.' Could

I possibly send a fax including a biography, a CV, a budget, four local and two international references, twelve hi-res color pictures of the locality, a floor plan, a safety record and a medical health certificate, along with a full description of the Promessa and the politics of its performative and socio-spatial coordinates, its epistemological *raison d'être*, its post-, anti- or subcolonial positioning, and a signed document stating that 50 per cent of all monetary profit over the next four years would be transferred to the Zurich I-CON as compensation for its overhead costs.

'And by the way, Dr Christenhuber will be on Arte this coming Wednesday, in case you're interested.'

Alright mate how are things? You're not writing back but I'll give it another try. Keep thinking back to those good old days and I wonder what's become of you. Since writing you last I went to Laos which was realy nice and "chilled", as they say, then Vietnam which was more hectic, then Cambodia which I was not realy prepared for, lots of poverty and amputees due to the recent history. Plus I got food poisoning and got stranded minus cash in a monsoon-drenched seaside resort four hours on a dirt road with insane moped driver away from nearest bank. Probably the first time I thought what the fuck am I doing here. Plus missed two flights so far through being too relaxed with check-in times. Was offered a night with this 17 year old I met but to my surprise I declined the offer, it was just soo easy, one days flirting and voila. But also I was mashed on Tequila slammers at the time. Next to Malaysia which is totally and utterly different again, especialy the east coast which is more strictly Islamic. Went to amazing islands called perhentains, and went to nice beach there, very "chilled", diving, snorkeling, 43 degrees, turtles, nature, ahhhh, I am a hippie really, despite my age. Drawback: being stared at like a zoo animal everywhere there. Now on west coast in Penang. more chinese and Indians with fantastic food, can't stop eating. Going to see a Bollywood film called Shakti tonight. Have taken so many pictures but not developed them yet but secretly think they will be exhibited internationally as shining examples of untrained photographic brilliance, a natural eye that captures the essence of a moment so pure, using only the cheapest cameras known to man. Mosquitos are a fucker and they love me. But discovered that tiger balm eases the sting completely. Bought two tailored suits in Vietnam and had them shipped to Oz by slave children on rowing boats. Difficult to have wanks here, especially since so many bronzed bodies around and so few masturbation opportunities. Feel like instead of sweating, will secrete spunk soon. Take care. Your one and only Uncle Tan

Tan Christenhuber was first introduced to the family when I was barely eight. I quickly grew to enjoy Tan's company far more than that of my friends and classmates, not to mention that of my parents. I admired the stark contrast between the snow-white hair and the dark tan, and the way his skin wrinkled into countless creases and folds as he smiled and told stories about the St Pauli red light district, or about the gun-toting, single male Norwegians of Minnesota, or the Olero Creek oil plant: all the corrupt officials, the slothful workers and their screaming housewives, who keep threatening to occupy the oil fields, 'get it all back now-now'.

'*Diese fetten afrikanischen Mamas*', he'd say, 'I bet you they'll do it. Perhaps not now-now, but sooner or later they will – and hey – who can blame them? Whooo can blame 'em? Their oil. Hey guys, we're only here to help you tap this stuff until you can do it yourself. But the bottom line is: their oil, not ours.'

When Zsa Zsa first paid us a visit in West Africa, I remember passionately impressing upon her what a generous, wonderful man Uncle Tan was. 'The only cool friend you guys have. I like him more than Mom and Dad and you and everyone else put together.'

Upon which she looked at me sternly from above her reading glasses, saying we should never trust 'them', that there was a Nazi in 'every one of them', and that she'd prove this to me in due course. Shortly after which she invited Tan and his German colleagues from the oil plant to an informal dinner, serving them beef stroganoff in Colman's mustard powder and Merlot, with steamed red cabbage in cumin and grape vinegar. After the *crème brûlée* for dessert, I watched Zsa Zsa empty one imported Zuger schnapps after another, teasing the men as she drank, 'You're being outdrunk by a female, a meek and humble Oriental woman, you do realize? What would your buddies say if they saw you now?'

Just as I was nodding off to sleep on my chair next to Tan's, Zsa Zsa started singing the *Hitlerjugend* ditties she'd learned back in occupied Paris. *Blonde und braune Buben passen nicht in die Stuben. Buben, die müssen sich schlagen, müssen was Tollkühnes wagen. Buben, sie sind von herrischer Art, Sturmvögel gleich ihre fröhliche Fahrt.* By the end of the evening, the engineers are screaming Hitlerian ballads, tears streaming down the creases of Tan's suntanned cheeks. *Deutschland, du wirst leuchtend stehn, mögen wir auch untergehn.* Zsa Zsa was watching me as she sang.

After a long afternoon nap, I decide to call Tarofi and invite him out to lunch at Bol Bol Burgers again. Surely he'd be curious and grateful to hear about Zurich and Marguerite Duras, the I-CON secretary and the Shiite society, but Tarofi grimly refers to 'urgent neighborhood business' and 'crisis meetings' and says he doesn't have the time, though perhaps next week, or after the Promessa opening. He doesn't seem interested in Christenhuber, nor in Zurich, and has already heard of the Shiite Society on the Förrlibuckstrasse.

'They're only about three dozen devotees. Maximum. But they're constantly begging and pleading for more and more funds. The guy, *Pishraft*, that cleric with the glasses, he calls the Tehran offices at least once a week.' The foundation, Tarofi explains, had never been successful at making themselves heard, let alone gaining respect among the key players in the Tehran network.

'Anyway, it's not very interesting. But there was something else. Just listen to this. I'm doing all this research, gender studies research, as they say, and I found this book on women in medieval Christianity. Late-medieval European Christianity. Listen. Did you know that in medieval England the women were veiled? Are you listening? I mean, they all had to wear these head garments in public, you know? And then there were these women who shaped their *hejabs* into horns. They'd stuff them with wigs. And others had tails they attached to their dresses and dragged along behind them in the street, and these bishops would condemn them as devils' nets that lure and destroy the souls of men and all that.'

'I had no idea.' I grab a cigarette, light it, stub it out again.

'Neither did I. Listen.' Tarofi starts reading aloud in his jagged English. '"In the woman wantonly adorned to capture souls, the garland upon her head is as a single coal or firebrand of Hell to kindle men with that fire." A firebrand of Hell to kindle men with that fire! And this bishop, this guy, he offered special pardons to anyone who harassed and humiliated the girls in public. It was the adornments, the *zeynat* itself, see, not the exposure of flesh, that got them going. "They put on their head hair that is not their own or unnatural color on their face. For, to put hair on the head or give a new complexion is the special concern of God.'"

I'm having trouble concentrating on the conversation. As I stare out the window at the dusty drizzle over the Karaj freeway, I can hear the plumbing chirping at me through the bathroom door.

'And this bishop keeps insisting how, when Christ was nailed to the cross, he was naked. Or this: "Even Mary, which hadde a premynence, above all women, in Bedlem whan she lay, at Crystys birthe no gret dispence, she wered a kovercheef, hornes wer cast away."

'Might be fun doing that at the opening. All these women in horns and tails and stuff.' There's a brief pause at the other end of the line.

'Dress them up in horns? What on earth for? Like a carnival? This is gender research, do you realize that?'

'Of course I do. It was just an idea. You know there's this historical re-enactment festival in Isfahan, and, I mean –'

'I shouldn't be reading you this stuff. Puts the wrong ideas in your head. Go do your installations or something. I'm serious.'

I start telling him about the Komplett Bar, thinking it might spark his curiosity, but Tarofi only half-heartedly teases me again, what a true Oriental macho romantic you are, then insists he really has very little time.

'Crisis meeting in half an hour. Serious row at the National Library. They discovered six prostitutes who were working in the men's lavatory.'

'What does that have to do with you?'

'I'm known for my sense of diplomacy. And my respect for human rights. You know they invited me to the Human Rights Conference in Rotterdam? And now I've been summoned to mediate between the library staff, the Women's League, the neighborhood elders, the police, the district militia and the municipality. A true challenge, believe me. They all have rights, you know, the prostitutes, the staff, the neighborhood elders. You should drop by if you have the time. Learn something useful.'

With the Afghani foreman calling me every twenty minutes, and the interior designer texting me night and day to complain about lacking materials and the slow speed of the handiwork, I have no time to read Stella's latest emails in my inbox, so I print them out and leave them on the coffee table, resolving to read them at the next possible moment. I spend the entire day drafting a fitting description of the Promessa, between phone calls from the designers, the plumbers, the Baltimore Muslim, who wishes to double her fee, the Zahedan anorexic, the various caterers, electricians, lighting technicians and some aspiring local artists. But also from Tarofi, who now calls at least twice a day, to reassure me repeatedly that I 'really had nothing to fear any longer'.

The I-CON secretary calls once again from the I-CON, to enquire whether I had any goddamn idea what 'responsibility' meant. 'We've already mentioned you to AVANTI, you know. Dr Christenhuber has got credit with these people. Credit and credibility. Credit and credence. Credit and confidence. And you've got to live up to that. He's not going to squander it just because of some artworld punk.'

I hastily copy and paste a patchwork of texts off the web, including a careful selection of excerpts from the Aglutinador, two major museum spaces in London, and a Deleuzian art collective in Istanbul, not to mention the *National Geographic* and the Al-Houda Islamic website. By way of local references, I devise a university professor, an established art critic, a dissident intellectual and a statement from Cyrus Rahati, while as international backing, I draw up letters of support from Tarofi and Camille Paglia. Stella once mentioned she knew Camille well and that they regularly went deep-sea fishing together, somewhere off Cape Cod. After a moment's hesitation, I include the column in the *Lufthansa Gazette*, along with a profile which appeared in the *Singapore Times*, Photoshopping it to replace the Aglutinador's logo with the Promessa's.

> You may think the Promessa collective will produce pretentious, adolescent toss. But you can't deny their position is bold and tackles big themes. Their work is juicy rather than dry. It may be crap, it may be derivative, but it doesn't fall into a neat division of concept versus craft. The Promessa collective laughs at the idea that craft has an inherent moral integrity by mastering a number of traditional arts and crafts – drawing and engraving, the diorama and wood carving – without claiming to be doing anything so crass as 'expressing themselves'. It was western modernism that exploited tribal art, tearing it out of context to make it the vessel of primitivism. Making their

own pastiche primitivism show and mutating it into an image of capitalism – I think Marx's theory of commodity fetishism is in here somewhere – the Promessa founders are going to have a lot of people's hackles rising. Mine included. But then, western exhibitions decontextualise and make a travesty of ethnographic art anyway. Surely it is this that creates kitsch. The Promessa is just the messenger. This is the kind of thing the artworld ought to be showing – it would create a row not about the tedious issue of Third World art good or bad, but about colonialism, capitalism, racism, the responsibilities of art and the evil of banality. At the very least, the Promessa is akin to a superior bullshit artist.

The official Promessa vernissage is drawing to a close. I've just finished my opening address and lean back against the wall near the entrance, taking in the scenery. The curators, editors, critics, clerics, bureaucrats and local artists are standing around in small groups among the folding tables generously stocked with Parsi Cola, Fanta, concentrated orange juice and alcohol-free beer, the visitors stepping daintily back and forth as they chew on the catered meat pastries, to avoid the falling crumbs. A predictable number of women at the opening, and a surprising number of men, have undergone nose-jobs, leaving them with petite nasal slopes pointing skyward.

A handful of visitors are still perusing the Promessa manifesto in English, which is the first thing you see as you emerge from the meandering entrance corridor, inscribed in gold paint across the brute concrete background of an entire wall. Most of the other walls are bare, offering little more than their varying shades of dusky white or concrete gray, while the horizontal strips of designer neon contrast meaningfully with the tribal pillows and the miniatures.

The terrarium, though missing out on rodents, is already alive with geckos, iguanas, lizards, chameleons and a hummingbird, along with several lories and lorikeets. Carefully placed throughout the gallery are the polypropylene lamps, acrylic tables, chandeliers, various breeds of seating arrangements.

Gracing one wall are the SAC paintings, which have turned out precisely as I'd hoped. A wedding dress rental agency bathed in neon, a shop window filled with soccer paraphernalia, a butcher's shop with lamb's heads piled up like tangerines, a mural announcing WE SHALL MAKE AMERICA SO ANGRY IT SHALL CHOKE ON ITS RAGE, a dentist's waiting room, the Bol Bol Burger branch in Elahie – all in the simple yet pensive, hopeful yet melancholy brushstroke suggesting the true subaltern. In the opposite corner of the room, by the entrance, the militia's contribution looks even more convincing in its grainy naivety flickering across a Sony plasma screen.

I had no choice but to call off the readings altogether, for Stella refused to reconsider, the Baltimore Muslim had now tripled her fee, and the crime novelist, having realized that Tarofi was somehow involved, announced he'd cooperate only if allowed a three-and-a-half-hour recital of dissident poetry.

I had contacted Ideal Standard in Lausanne just in time to change the exhibition title, and 'Violence of Discourse, Discourse of Violence: Mapping the Post-Epistemic Dismemberment of Sheharazade' became 'If You're Going Through Hell, Keep Going', which, as the designers agreed, offered a comfortable common ground between the transvestite and the *bassijis* and generally 'worked well' for a gallery opening.

My opening address was politely polemic and vaguely confrontational, leading through a carefully packaged constellation of points and themes which, I argued, underlay any contemporary discussion of international art and culture. Ranging from Palestine to the laughable European media landscape and its tragic misconceptions of contemporary African art, to the issue of resistance in the age of mechanical reproduction and on to the challenges of 'mapping the urban memoria' of Tehran, ending with a string of delightful family anecdotes on the Promessa opening back in May 1963. Rock Hudson, Georgian gypsy songs, Maoists, Leninists, Trotskyists, Stalinists, 'Third Way' Communists, Social Democrats.

I was, however, disappointed to learn that the creator of the 'Sleep of a Thousand Destinies (Minus One)' piece had emigrated to Tokyo. According to the artist's tutor at the Academy, he was hoping to find work on a construction site, but was currently selling counterfeit telephone cards behind Harajuku station and was living under a bench in Yogi Park. I considered a webcam consultation with the émigré, entitled '*Cada artista que se va es un fragmento que se pierde*' but decided against it, mainly for lack of time, and opting instead for something more theatrical and effective.

Following my carefully impertinent curatorial address, I was joined in the spotlight by an Afghani laborer in his mauve uniform who had taken part in the Promessa renovations from the very beginning. I lay my arm around his shoulder and put on a supportive smile. 'And so how are we tonight, young fellow?' The crowd moved a little closer around the two of us. 'How about a word for our guests?'

'Good evening, honorable ladies and gentlemen.' The melodious Afghani accent became even more endearing as the worker trembled with stage fright, and the audience broke out in a good-natured, breezy chuckle. 'As a matter of fact, I actually have three things I wish to tell you. First of all. Don't cry, work! Second –'

He was interrupted by laughter. 'Second,' he continued, pointing to himself, '*ceci n'est pas un antifasciste!*' and was met once again with appreciative giggles and a lively rush of clapping and whistling. Some of the audience was already familiar with the manifesto, already whispering the last point. 'Third. *Las instituciones son una mierda.*'

Upon which I took a step back, away from the Afghani, looking him up and down slowly, taking on an affected, theatrical posture I'd carefully practiced in front of my bathroom mirror the night before. 'Something is bothering you, my friend. I can tell.'

The Afghani sighed and shrugged his shoulders. 'Can I tell you something? After telling you what I have to say, I believe I shall have to resign immediately.'

He looked at the crowd, turning his back to me. The lights were dimmed as dry ice started lapping at our feet, oozing from a portable device installed just behind us. I threw my hands in the air, in mock despair. 'Oh no!'

'What's wrong?'

'You will give up this post? I thought you were happy here.

186

You have a secure income here.'

'You are about to understand. You will understand the moment I tell you about all this crap that's been going on. Believe me, your first word of advice will be: "Resign!"'

'Well, we'll see about that.'

'Sir! You're always on my mind! I believe I'm actually in love with you. And so I need things that remind me of you. That is the only thing that calms me down, and so I steal things from you all the time. Things that are lying around. I mean, not just things that are lying around, but money as well.'

'That's a sweet way of putting it. So you're stealing money from me? Could it be that you simply want it for yourself?'

'What? The money?' The Afghani trembled with shock and dismay. The spectators slowly warmed to the stiff, clumsy play-acting unfolding before them, sniggering and whispering to each other.

'Yes. Precisely. I mean, fine, but normally, people in your situation steal personal belongings. I mean, you're not trying to tell me that when you steal credit cards or cash, the stuff reminds you of me?'

'Yes I am. That way, you're always with me.' He placed one hand on his heart.

'Stop these stupid excuses. You stole from me.' I started shaking with fury. 'You have *robbed me*!'

'But only because I wanted to be with you always.'

'Why does misery always have to beat a path *to my door*? *Why is this so*? I pulled out a small handgun from my pocket, placed it against the Afghani's brow and pulled the trigger. At the sound of the gun going off, the Afghani slumped to the floor, and three

Afghanis in mauve uniforms stepped in with chiffons and pails of water. They soaked up the sticky red rivulets criss-crossing the marble floor, barely visible through the thick dry ice, laying their colleague on a long sheet of transparent plastic and dragging him away by his rubber workboots. The audience, unsure of what had just happened, settled for being visibly disappointed by the abrupt ending to the script and began to disperse.

When I was later asked for the title of this inaugurational gesture – a question I'd been eagerly expecting – I said I was still hesitating between 'Double Negative' and 'The Day Our Enemies Praise Us We Shall Mourn'. The dialogue was actually stolen, *tel quel*, from an avant-garde Berlin playwright named Pollesch, but no one at the Promessa would have known him, let alone recognized the text, and it wouldn't make much difference if they had.

A group of young artists in running shoes and Armani shirts have now gathered around the editor of *Ordak*, debating Mehrangiz's recent work.

'It's quite good in some ways. The compositions are very clever, for example. Powerfully vulnerable, in a way.'

'If you see it in the dark, wearing extra-dark Ray Bans, I hear it's fine.'

'She's moving to New York or something. They're all leaving. It's typical. Soon as you have a name, off you go. No responsibility, no nothing.'

'Exactly. There's no responsibility, no shame, no nothing.' someone echoes.

'But that's the same everywhere. Western art is just as apolitical.

It's globalization. Why get pissed off about something when you can just get up and go somewhere else?'

'Exactly. Globalization makes you apolitical. Because basically mobility makes you apolitical.' I spot two teenage girls from the Zirzamin Debating Club trying to peer over people's shoulders as they listen in on the conversation. Nearby is a small flock of mullahs, including Tarofi, once again surrounded by his many sons, wearing his Kojak sunglasses and a dark-brown camel-fur cape over a second cape of light-blue transparent tunic.

I walk over to vigorously shake Tarofi's hand, and he looks delighted to see me, croaking excitedly, very good nice. I offer him a small list of platitudes expressing submissive, boundless gratitude and am introduced to three more clergymen, *khoshbakhtam khoshbakhtam*, after which I clutch Tarofi by the sleeve and pull him away from his colleagues.

'So how is your gender research going?'

Tarofi looks slightly pale and keeps tensing his jaw, a glistening layer of sweat on his forehead, his vaguely Iberian features not as virile as usual. He leans over and mumbles something into my ear. 'My dear, we need to go over something, I'm worried about you.' But I'm not in the mood for last-minute reassessments or second thoughts of any kind, and take to berating the Afghanis for making a mess of the bloodstains. 'It's all over the place. Get a proper mop, for God's sake. A mop. You know what a mop is?'

I watch them stow away the tables, mop the floor once again and rearrange the furniture, then take a cab home, having just enough time to shower and change into the Zahedan three-piece before driving back for the second opening.

From the bathroom window, I glance over to the apartment in block 43D, empty once again, ever since the day of the unexpected Polaroid tea ceremony. I look myself over in the mirror, shower for the third time that day, then seek out my saffron-yellow shirt and choose a pair of fly-shaped pink sunglasses, then change my mind and wear my Porsche Veron 1 instead. I mould my hair – usually dark red, or a murky auburn according to the season, now almost orange in the bright sunlight flowing in through the bathroom window – into a Ceasar's, shape my eyebrows into two clean arches with a tweezer, apply two different skin creams to two particular parts of my face, hands and feet and, after a moment's hesitation, decide not to shave, but dab some *Ladjevardi* aftershave on my neck and wrists.

I walk over to the TV and spend several minutes staring absent-mindedly at Larry King interviewing Tarik Aziz, before switching to Balkan Bang and a wide-angle shot of a chubby peroxide blonde masturbating with a carrot in a muddy wheelbarrow, squinting in the sunlight, clenching a long stalk of wheat between her teeth. I wonder whether it might be appropriate to arrive at the opening an hour late, the guests noticing my casual entrance, smiling and nonchalant, so serene and satisfied with the way things are going generally. Then again, I have yet to adjust the equalizer on the sound system, pay off the traffic cops on Palestine Street, and prepare the opium pipe for the back garden. Cyrus, meanwhile, is to introduce me to a dealer, so I can offer a line or two to a select handful of guests. A line with Neil Diamond, though in some ways hardly worth the money, might well be the only chance I have against Zsa Zsa and Rock Hudson, with his imitation gold Rolex, or the Bulsaras with their Kir Royales and honey-roasted peanuts.

I stand up to call a cab, and it is only now that I notice the message panel of my answering machine, blinking impatiently. The first message is from Zsa Zsa, saying that, at the end of the day, she 'could not, would not, and indeed should not' come to the opening, it was too emotional, 'simply too much, *tout court*. I don't know what to tell you, my dear.' Her voice is hoarse and slightly shaky. I can hear her pausing to light a cigarette, and picture her wagging her ivory walking cane from side to side as she exhales the smoke from her Gauloise. 'I'm not sure it's a good idea. Sorry. I just think it would be a bad idea somehow.'

At this moment I distinctly hear a voice in the background but cannot make out what it's saying. 'And I do love you, my dear,' she adds. 'Never forget that.'

Though relieved by Zsa Zsa's decision, I'm slightly annoyed nonetheless, not only by the murmuring in the background but by something in the tone of her voice which I cannot quite put my finger on. The following two messages are both from the I-CON, reprimanding me for not including their overhead costs in my budget, insisting that Dr Christenhuber had 'never heard of any Camille Paglia' and demanding to know whether 'this woman' was some kind of fabrication, 'some cheap rip-off, I just hope for your sake that she isn't.'

In her second message, the I-CON secretary says the chairman of AVANTI had expressed grave doubts regarding the Promessa and was threatening to call off the project, indeed Dr Christenhuber had been 'considering it all day'. Just as I delete the messages my phone rings. 'Tarofi here. Hope I'm not bothering you.'

'Not in the slightest.' I switch off the TV and check my watch.

'What's new?'

'Well, listen. It's not nice to be the bringer of bad news. Especially if it's opening night and everything. But, well.' He pauses. '*Hail not a messenger of crime or comfort, for the message alone is worthy of judgement.* Your beloved Kalegondeh, right?'

'I guess so.'

'Wrong, darling. It's Rumi. But anyway. Listen. I thought you should know that Stella will be in Tehran later on tonight. Just thought you might want to know.' I only now remember Stella's emails lying on the coffee table, still unread.

'You know what? I guessed as much.' I walk over to the printouts, fold them twice and slip them into my jacket.

'Perhaps you should be careful.'

'Perhaps.'

'Just as long as you know she'll be here. And I also wanted you to know for a fact that I'm very happy with you and that I want you to keep going. Very nice good,' he chortles. 'I'm just worried. It seems there have been some complications here and there.'

I thank him for calling, throwing in three or four platitudes of gratitude and devotion, as I check my hair, which is getting a touch too long for a Ceasar's. I consider combing it into a classic side parting, but decide against it.

Musing over my newfound friendship with what was once a roving clerical henchman, I remember a particularly heartrending propaganda slogan on the walls of the Zirzamin *bassiji* headquarters – THE DAY OUR ENEMIES PRAISE US WE SHALL MOURN – realizing I'd long stopped considering Tarofi an enemy or even a threatening presence of any kind. Tarofi has actually taken to me, rather enthusiastically at that, and I wonder whether this has any relation to – or bearing on – Stella's intentions with regard to me.

The air outside block 44D is unusually humid. Once again, the cab driver is the young Brezhnev in the light gray suit. I'm surprised by the silence in the car. 'Not into Neil Diamond any longer?'

Brezhnev clicks on the radio without bothering to answer the question. The state radio is playing an instrumental, keyboard version of Shakira's 'Whenever, Wherever', a drum computer playing a gentle, tapping rhythm in the background. As we approach Azadi Boulevard, we see a traffic jam stretching out for several miles ahead. The taxi comes to a complete halt next to a teenage couple in a bright orange BMW, smoking weed and listening to psychedelic Goa Techno at full volume, drowning out the tender, instrumental tune in our cab. I start tilting my head back and forth in different directions, trying to relax my neck muscles as I'd watched the Arabs do in Zurich last week.

An hour later, the BMW is two cars behind us, the only indication of any movement whatsoever. I recount the remaining practicalities in my mind, hoping Cyrus will take care of the cocaine without any further reminder on my part, and remember I should leave the Promessa to pick up Dr Christenhuber at Mehrabad airport, around 1 AM. I attempt to distract myself with small talk. 'Colin Powell. What a pimp,' I venture.

'Yes, well, you know.' The driver sighs. A similar sigh to the *bassiji* officer's. Sighing, I conclude, wishing I had my notebook, is an essential, integral part of everyday Persian rhetoric. Usually followed by 'but that's the way it is', 'dear God, what have we done to deserve this' and other expressions of bittersweet, composed exasperation.

'To tell you the truth, I wish they'd just come over. Bomb the hell out of everything, get it over with. So we can finally relax. *Rahat shim, vallah*.' He sighs.

'I see what you're saying, but what can you do?' I offer, noticing a new neon sticker on the dashboard, just next to the tape recorder. 'Fresh Your Feeling' it says, in happy letters of blue and orange.

'Just wait and see what's happening in Afghanistan,' Brezhnev is saying. 'Foreign investments coming out their ears. Ten years from now, they'll overtake us. Wagging DVDs and Longines and Rolexes in our faces. What a disgrace.' The driver sighs, lights a *Bahman*, rolls down the window, sighs again and cranks up the radio. A woman is now reciting sticky-sweet hymns of praise for the revolution to bouncy background beats that sound very much like Yazoo. 'Our world-famous revolution, budding forth like a February flower, a glorious manifestation of love,' she croons.

I run my hand over the bump on my chest, tracing the outlines of Stella's email in my inside pocket, then pull it out and slowly unfold the pages. The driver clicks off the radio, and grins. 'Are you Christian?'

'You know what I tell Christians?' the driver continues without waiting for my answer, 'I tell them: "Look. Listen to me."' As he speaks, Brezhnev bends forward and gesticulates over his steering wheel, as if the Christians in question had clambered onto the hood and were staring at him through the windscreen. "Listen. When you buy a computer, you get the newest model, right? Like when you buy a car, you do exactly that. Why get an old Volkswagen if you can have a new Nissan Patrol? Same goes for prophets. Islam is the latest revelation, not the Bible. Bible's six hundred years older."'

I take a moment to think this over. 'But some people prefer older models.'

'That's their problem, not mine.'

Closing

The A3 poster outside the Promessa gallery is an intricate medley of camouflage blotches, vertical stripes of varying width, and thickset letters saying WHEN YOURE GOING THROUGH HELL, KEEP GOING in Jordi Grotesk font. Palestine Street is filled with double-parked cars, and I can see more guests crawling up and down side alleys in Honda Civics and Range Rovers in search of a parking space.

As I yank open the door to the Promessa, old school South Central Hip Hop spills out on the street, with far too much bass, distorting the sound almost beyond recognition, causing a rasping noise with each beat, precisely as I'd expected. *Got my nuts on your tonsils.* In the stairway, the zebra stripes now replaced by a pale shade of mauve, I bump into Cyrus and Mina, the two of them arm in arm, taking their time on the way down. Cyrus's breath reeks of beer and tobacco. 'Stylishly late? That the idea?'

'Yes. Actually that is the idea. How nice to see the two of you.' Mina doesn't react. She's wearing her Metallica baseball cap backwards over her headscarf, light blonde strands stretching out horizontally in several directions, her Chloë perfume more penetrating than ever.

I brush past them to the gallery, where some sixty guests are helping themselves to the crystal flasks of raisin and date vodka, mixing the liquor with ice, sour cherry, grapefruit concentrate or Parsi Cola. Lined up next to the bottles are tiny ceramic bowls filled with pistachios, pickles, celery or olives in pomegranate. Two of the Afghanis are handing out glossy cardboard flyers featuring the Promessa manifesto, with hundreds of copies already lining the floor.

Mina and Cyrus are still lurching down the stairs in slow motion, stopping every few steps to discuss something outrageously amusing, producing a queue of visitors behind them. The tall woman behind Cyrus looks strangely familiar, and for a brief moment of intense panic I believe I recognize San, but the moment passes as I recognize the interior designer, grinning over at me, raising both hands in a thumbs up. By the time they reach the end of the stairway, Mina has begun filming Cyrus with a digital Sonycam from up close as he giggles, looks around, then announces something to the camera and slaps the interior designer on her behind. As she turns around angrily, Mina moves up to her, holding the camera up into her face.

'Cyrus, can I see you for a moment.'

'Sooooo!' Cyrus is still giggling. 'The host himself!'

'What happened to the coke?'

'The coke?' I turn around and make for the kitchen, where fresh herbs are being laid out on small silver platters, adding decorative touches to Russian salads, saffron rice cakes, eggplant dips, spinach in garlic yogurt, chicken Tah-chin, lamb kebab skewers, red peppers stuffed with split peas, minced beef with cinnamon, omelette slices with nuts and fenugreek, or turmeric and zucchini. The caterers, all in white Hugo Boss shirts and black 501s, start carrying the platters into the gallery.

Knock yo teeth outcha mouth cause my dick's gotta fit. As the kitchen door swings briefly open, I can hear the bass is still overtaxing the speakers, causing the same obnoxious grating sounds. I proceed to light the samovar, filling a ceramic bowl with spiky chunks of yellow, crystallized sugar, find an oblong ceramic platter and lay out two rows of jelly comfit and greasy caramel Sohan with pistachio brittle. Within a concealed drawer by the stove I find a wooden pipe and a round, bronze receptacle filled with ashes and chunks of charcoal.

The back garden of the Promessa is a pebbled square with two wooden cots covered in straw mats and handcrafted Baluchi pillows, surrounded by untended rose bushes on all sides. Burning at the far end of the square is a small fire, which one of the Afghanis has been tending to all evening. I'm pleased and almost touched, since I remember mentioning it only once, in passing, the day before. I toss the coals into the fire, light a cigarette and wait, scrubbing the charcoal off my palms with a handkerchief. In the distance, cars and motorbikes are driving up and down the side alleys around Palestine Street. Within a matter of hours, I realize, it will all be over, and the Promessa will have hopefully found the epic finale it deserves. I fan the fire with an embroidered Turkmen wafting flap, then withdraw the charcoal and lovingly place it on the bronze platter, forming a small, shimmering pyramid of ash-grey and glowing orange.

I can still feel the outlines of Stella's emails in my inside pocket. I really should be rereading them, just to make sure there's no misunderstanding. The first was sent two days ago. 'Listen no need to bother about Christenhuber's arrival, just be outside the venue at 1 AM. Due to the complications you've knowingly been causing you shall be executed by a shot to the head after the opening. I'm sorry. Stella.' The second email, written almost an hour later, says, 'Just kidding. Ha ha. XX S.'

Someone has just walked into the garden from behind me. 'Ah, yes, so what do we have here?'

I turn around to see the Chinese cultural attaché, talking to someone who looks very much like Neil Diamond. 'Opium. Naughty, naughty.'

He wags a forefinger up and down at me, then turns to the spitting image of Neil Diamond standing next to him. 'Neil! Shall we have a try? Have you ever tried?'

Diamond is smaller than I would have expected and is wearing a black dinner jacket with generous shoulder pads and a red T-shirt saying NO PASARAN in bright yellow font, his white jeans ending two inches above his ankles. He seems very moved by something, looking slowly back and forth between the rose bushes and the glowing charcoal, reaching out to pick a white rose from a nearby bush to slip it into the outside pocket of his jacket. I try to regain composure and stand up to greet them, still holding the bowl of crystallized sugar in one hand.

'Yes, and so this is the boy who takes care of this place,' the diplomat is saying, 'He's very sweet. And his English is really good.'

'I'm the founder. The host. This used to belong to, that is, it was run by –'

'That's right. And I'm sure you wouldn't mind if we let Neil, mind if I call you Neil, if we let Neil have a first taste of opium, no? First cut is the deepest – baby I know. Love that song. Was that your first big hit?' He walks over to one of the cots and lies down on his side, expertly propping himself up on one elbow. 'See, let me show you. You make yourself nice and comfy, then you stick a *liiiiiittle* bit of this, *tariyak* they call it, sounds like Teriyaki right? Teriyaki chicken? Anyway you stick it *riiiiight* here on the pipe by the hole here on top.'

Diamond walks over to him, undecided, turns around and takes a brief, suspicious look at me, then sits down on the edge of the other cot, opposite the Beijing diplomat.

'So Neil, tell me, what does Farsi sound like to you?'

'Well.' Diamond watches the diplomat as he curls a chunk of opium into a tiny ball and sticks it unto the pipe. 'Like a Jesuit walking through a rose garden. Who pricks his finger on the thorn of a rose and apologizes profusely to the flower.'

In the kitchen, I take a flask of raisin vodka from the bar counter, fill a small glass and drink it straight, then immediately fill another. After which I light a Golden Super Love Standard and walk over to the door, from where I can comfortably watch the guests. Mina is still pointing her DV camera at Cyrus, who drunkenly greets whoever happens to pass by, boisterously drawing people into conversations by which they are visibly irritated as they frown and walk off, causing both Cyrus and Mina to giggle uncontrollably.

The Promessa is filling up with heavily perfumed men and women in spanking new running shoes or dizzyingly high heels, most of them reaching for the stuffed peppers and meat skewers. Below the antique mirrorball, small groups of three or four have now started dancing, while others are sitting on Turkmen pillows near the entrance, smoking weed or cigarettes. The Cuban ambassador arrives, bringing with him his twin daughters, rowdy nine-year-olds in matching polo shirts and knee socks.

They walk over to me to offer a gift, two Meadow Jumping Chipmunks for the terrarium, Pilar and Pepita, named after the two girls themselves. The ambassador looks very pleased, smiling at his kids as he gyrates his hips to the music. *Cause if you fuck with me you fuckin with death row*. A number of news correspondents, most of them prominent liberal voices from within the news establishment, are sitting around the Eames surfboard tables with various cultural attachés and local photojournalists.

Huddling in front of the piece on the Sony plasma screen are some art critics and curators based in London and Copenhagen, trying to look apocalyptic, enthusiastic and nonchalant at the same time as the camera zooms up to a white lily, rapidly slipping in and out of focus. At one point, between two Hip Hop tracks, I make out the phrase 'voices of a quickly disappearing world'.

Mina, drunker than ever, suddenly grabs me by the wrist, generous smudges of makeup on her cheeks, and hanging from her eyelashes in tiny black blobs. 'Everything OK? You look *booooored*, man.'

'No, everything OK.' I push past her towards the restrooms, in the hope of finding someone to share a line of coke with, opening the bathroom door to see Hare Rama Schröder seated on the sink, eyes shut, leaning back against the mirror. Someone is on his knees with his face buried between her legs, causing her to shiver and possibly moan, but I cannot hear her, thanks to the music and the rasping, granular bassline. I'm reminded, once again, of Cyrus's erotic punchline, panties are jackpot, and glance down at the man on the floor, then back at Rama Schröder, who has opened her eyes and is looking straight at me.

It's past midnight, and Cyrus is standing near the entrance with a celebrity pop theorist from Vienna whose name escapes me. The celebrity theorist is smoking a cigarette in a self-conscious, sideways manner *Vogue Homme International* would presumably term 'artistic', wearing a white suit of immaculate fit, his hair combed into a faultless side parting, making me regret the decision of sticking to my Ceasar's. If Hamburg Türknet cashiers are wearing Ceasars, it may be time for a change.

I overhear someone on the other side of the circular bar reciting a Kalegondeh courtship ballad to someone wearing a BUCK FUSH baseball cap. *You and I/ Together a silent voice/ United in our separation/ You and I.*

A small crowd of art students are standing nearby, clustered around a photographer whom I remember from the communist intelligentsia retreat in Beirut. 'So you're actually saying that, like, the Syrians have massacred more Palestinians than the Israelis.'

'Well all I said was that it's quite possible.'

'Why does everything have to be so complicated? I mean I

just couldn't care less. I'm not getting into this. Fuck this political shit, man.'

'No but basically it's simple. Everyone goes for the Palestinians, right? I mean that's basically it, right?'

'This party's too much. Let's go to Aqua, no? Take our friend and go to Aqua.'

'What's Aqua?'

'Aqua. It's a café place full of aquariums, even the outside façade is an aquarium, and the tables are cubic tanks full of exotic fish and seaweed and stuff. And you just watch them through the glass tabletop and have a Nescafé or a banana milk shake, or whatever.'

'Relaxing place. Really a relaxing place. You can meditate, let yourself go, let your thoughts flow, actually kind of spiritual, you know?'

'So did you know Michael Moore is here?

'Michael Moore? Where?

'The guy by the stairs. The fat guy.'

'That's not Michael Moore.'

'Of course it's Michael Moore. Course it's Michael Moore.'

'Oh my God, yeah you're right. It's Michael Moore. Is it?'

Standing by the stairway, we can see Mehrangiz chatting excitedly with Michael Moore and Bono, all of them draped in black and white Palestine neckscarves. Not exactly Rock Hudson and Queen Farah, but gratifying nonetheless. 'Going *on* and *on* and ON,' Mehrangiz is happily screaming at her audience, 'it's, like, *lady*, please stop piling all those *adjectives* on *top* of each other.'

Someone of perhaps seventy years of age, in a khaki suit with a white kerchief sticking out of his breast pocket, is standing alongside, watching me. He nods and smiles as he catches my eye, and immediately starts crossing the room. I cannot decide whether to wait or walk away, and by the time I opt for the latter it's too late, the man already shouting into my ear to make himself heard over the musical backdrop, which is still decidedly West Coast. *My dick runs deep so deep so deep put her ass to sleep.*

'I know your parents. And your grandfather, too. I met them right here,' he jabs a long finger downwards, at the ground beneath them. 'Promessa, Tehran, 1968.'

'You did.'

'And I know your grand-aunt Zsa Zsa. A great woman. A true lady in every sense of the word. Quite a temper. But a true lady always. Honor came first. Always. And such wonderful tits. And so many stories about her. Do you know the tank story?'

'Yes, as a matter of fact I believe I do.' Walking past us, towards the liquor flasks, still arguing intently, the visiting curators interrupt their disagreement as they see me, to offer a friendly smile and cordially raise their glasses in a toast.

'Ah. I must tell you that story.'

'I said I already know that story.'

'Your grand-aunt was courting this gentleman. Armenian. Beautiful smile, well-educated, exquisite dress, and very well-hung, or so they say. And a member of the Armenian Club. And one day, they start calling him a "swine". Imagine. They call him a swine because he's going out with "a Muslim whore". Imagine that. A Muslim whore. So what happens? Your grand-aunt finds out. So you can imagine. And you know what she does? She gets a tank. One of those big old army tanks the Shah was buying from the Americans, by the truckload. By the hundreds. Thousands.'

Over at the DJ table, Cyrus and Hare Schröder get into a playful scuffle over the music, and Ice Cube's *Predator* LP comes to an abrupt stop, plunging the room into a barrage of shrieks, giggles and sluggish conversation.

I briefly consider intervening when I realize with a slight panic that it's already past 1 AM. I walk across the floor, breathing deeply, take the winding corridor to the entrance and step out on the sidewalk. As the door swings shut behind me, I can hear the bassline resume its course below. I cross the street, open the back door of a metallic-grey BMW X-5 and take a seat.

About five seconds pass in the dark of the leather-padded interior until someone at the steering wheel reaches back and clicks on the overhead light. Next to me is a slender man whom I recognize as the Shekufeh interrogator. He's dressed in an eighties drape suit by Alan Flusser, with natural shoulders, a full chest and peaked lapels. 'So how is everything. Is the party any good?' The driver is looking into the rear-view mirror, smiling at me. I don't react.

'Never mind. You know I was wondering about something. Tell me. Have you been to the Khomeini museum up in Jamaran?'

He only briefly waits for an answer. 'Well, you should go. Even Castro went, he went last week. Especially if you like galleries and all that. Beautifully done. You see his furniture, his clothes, his perfume, his paintings, all sorts of stuff.' He sighs. 'So anyway. All things considered, I have to say we were pretty happy with you. We all were. Stella, everyone.'

There's still no reaction on my part, which doesn't seem to surprise the driver, who now turns around to look me in the eye. 'I especially liked your appearance in Shekufeh. You pretty much got everything right. Toptabulosa. I liked that a lot.' I look out the window. Two doors down from the Promessa is a boutique with an oversized wooden signboard, with red lettering saying *KYF O KAFSH ROMANTYK*. The driver turns back and starts talking at the windshield, much like the young Leonid Brezhnev only a few hours earlier.

'The Hamburg Zurich Beirut thing is working out nicely too.' He pauses. 'Will take a while, but that's OK. Let's remember that St Petersburg took longer than expected, but it was worth the wait, as we all know. The only thing is, well. The only thing is, you shouldn't have done that signature business in Shekufeh. You know that.'

I look up to see whether the driver is watching me, but he's still staring straight ahead, at the Nissan parked in front of us. 'And also: you could have checked back with us about the San thing before you went ahead. The San thing, you know? You should have checked back.'

The interrogator in Alan Flusser clears his throat and nods, agreeing with the driver. 'Exactly. And the other thing is you never passed on the check.' He checks his watch. 'And it was all becoming very awkward because we were positive you'd tell Stella at some point. I mean it was such an obvious sort of situation, no? And then came the San thing.' He checks his watch again. 'About time, no?' He looks up at the eyes and eyebrows in the rearview mirror, then turns to me. 'You didn't flake out on this too, did you?'

'Any moment now,' I say, to no one in particular. The driver starts the car and slowly drives down the street, past boutiques and stores selling computer software, designer glasses or university textbooks. Which is when we feel the stifled thud of an underground blast, followed by a low-pitched muffled thump not far behind. As we turn right, into Enqelab Avenue, I fight the urge to turn back and see what is left of the Promessa.

As I step out of the car, I can see the lights are on in my apartment. The others remain seated as I walk up to the entrance of block 44D with familiar jarring movements in my stomach.

Stella is standing by the living-room window, wearing a shapeless, washed-out jogging suit, thick, rectangular glasses and a boyish crew cut. She has put on a considerable amount of weight since we last met, and I'm oddly touched, as if she'd done so just to please me. I smile nervously at Stella, who doesn't smile back, her now very globular cheeks lending her a vulnerable, almost pouting expression.

Our last meeting was well over a year ago, and there's a sense of embarrassed, misplaced intimacy in the air. After a moment's hesitation, Stella walks up to me and gently takes me by the arm, just above the elbow, leading me into the bathroom. I look down and notice that her fingers are no longer lovingly manicured as they used to be.

'You did a great job,' she's saying. 'And we hope you're as happy as we are.' Stella pauses as we reach the bathroom. 'I don't even care about the check that much. Only problem is, well, they have your signature now. That's unfortunate. Not that we don't trust you. Just a matter of policy. Why make things complicated, at this stage? I'm sure you understand?'

As I step inside she closes the door behind me, so I reach for the notebook in my inside pocket and take a seat on the edge of the bathtub. I never considered this situation to be an option in the overall scheme of things, although in retrospect, it makes perfect sense. At least the Promessa has found a worthy ending. Cruel and gracious, ambiguous and cutting, dramatic and humble at one and the same time.

At the very least, Stella could have framed another rooftop martyrdom, which might have been more fitting, more emblematic, given the Zirzamin context. But at this stage, the site-specific, suicide scenario looks quite unlikely. Staring out the window into the apartment opposite, I wonder where exactly she'll be placing the barrel of the handgun. Assuming it will be above my left sideburn, if I stand in the middle of the room facing the window, I'll be leaving the *Action Jackson* patterns on the mirror and shower curtain. Most of the liquid will be soaked up by the bathroom rug, and since the floor is slightly tilted, whatever is not contained by the fabric will flow neatly towards the bathtub, along the edges and into the drain, making faint chirping noises as it trickles down the spout. I shall place this notebook on the shelf by the face creams, where it won't get stained.

All the pastes and liquids in their respective tubes and flasks are neatly lined up, keenly anticipating their date of replacement, as always. I can hear Stella outside, taking her Polaroid portrait from the wall, gathering all the Zip discs, minidiscs, VHS tapes, newspaper articles, urban panoramas, email printouts and audio CDs she can find. But she'll probably leave our Moleskines where they are, piled on the floor by the Le Corbusier armchair.